GW00494395

Walking Through Time

A Novel

by

Lauren Walden Rabb

Lauren Walden Rabb

A Windswept Book
Windswept House Publishers
Mt. Desert, ME

Copyright Lauren Walden Rabb 1998
Library of Congress Catalog Number 98-60229
ISBN 1-883650-48-8

Cover: *"Clam Diggers, Annisquam" 1888*
Original oil by William Lamb Picknell
(American, 1853-1897)
Private Collection

Cover design: *State of the Art Graphics,*
Nashville, Tennessee

Printed in the United States of America
for the publisher by
Bang Printing

For David and Marisa

and
most of all

for Gertrude

Prologue

Annisquam, Cape Ann, Massachusetts 1883

Along the ridge of a hill overlooking the beach, a lone artist made his way toward the town of Annisquam, carrying an easel and paint box as he walked through the long shadows of early evening. He had spent all day concentrating, trying to "see" nature - to be one with his surroundings - and was now aware of a comfortable feeling of exhaustion from a good day's work. His mind was clear of conscious thought.

As he neared town, sounds of activity from the beach began floating up the hill. A buzz of excitement indicated that something unusual was occurring. When the noise reached the artist, he made his way to the edge of the ridge and peered down.

On a wide expanse of sand just a short distance below him, a baseball game was underway. Half the young men and boys of town were spread across the beach; the other half were congregated on a small group of rocks off to one side, waiting their turn at bat. On the other side of the "field," a larger group of rocks served as a grandstand for the townspeople. All attention at that moment was focused on home plate, where a young lady with a determined stance and a bat poised over her shoulder was waiting for her first pitch.

William Lamb Picknell, the twenty-nine year-old artist, recognized Gertrude Powers, his nineteen year-old neighbor.

The pitcher turned to look behind him, and with a toss of his head told his players to step back. The girl's teammates began chanting encouragement:

"C'mon Gertrude!"

"Show 'em what you got!"

"Look - they're scared already!"

From his spot on the hill, Picknell could see Gertrude's face twitch mischievously as she tried to swallow a smile. The men and women watching the game leaned forward expectantly.

The first pitch came in high, and the umpire called out "Ball!" Shouts of "Good eye!" and "Wait for the right one!" came from the restless crowd. A second pitch, low and outside, almost got away from the catcher.

"He's not going to walk her, is he?" wailed a young lady from the sidelines, as if that would be a disaster too awful to comprehend. The pitcher turned red and scowled, and the players on the field shifted their legs and released their breath.

Gertrude stepped away from the plate and knocked the bat against the sand, then stepped back and lifted the bat back over her shoulder. The pitcher glared at her. Then he wound up, and hurled a perfect pitch straight at her strike zone with all his might.

With one step and a mighty swing, Gertrude hit the ball. It flew high into the air like a soaring bird, and arced over the field, finally settling far away at the edge of the water. The center fielder scrambled after the ball while his teammates jumped up and down and shouted at him to hurry. The crowd cheered, and Gertrude raced around the bases. She was past third before the center fielder could throw the ball, and easily reached home as the ball came hurling in toward the catcher.

Teammates and spectators ran over to congratulate Gertrude, while Picknell, with a bemused expression, contemplated his neighbor:

"My God, she's a picture! I wish I could capture that sort of movement in my work. That would be a feat - like Degas' great paintings of ballerinas!"

He watched the girl laughing and skipping happily back to the sidelines, and, with a chuckle of his own, he turned and walked away.

Gertrude happened to look up just as Picknell moved off. The exuberant grin faded from her face, and became replaced with a wistful smile, which she carefully hid. Anyone catching her expression at that moment would have known that she wished to be up there with the artist, talking with him and hearing about his day, instead of playing baseball with a bunch of silly boys down on the beach.

1

1997

It was unusually warm for June in Annisquam, and the air was thick with the buzz of insects and the smell of salt. Eleanor pulled up the driveway and heard the sand crunching beneath the tires of her Buick. Although all the car windows were open, it had still been a miserable drive from the city. Her white cotton blouse stuck to her skin and her jeans felt glued to the seat.

Peter, fourteen years old and immune to discomfort, jumped out of the car with a whoop of joy and began running around the front yard, clamoring for her to give him the house key. She fished it out of her hot leather purse (*God, I should buy* a *summer bag*, she thought), and handed it over. Instantly Peter was up the porch steps and in the cottage, running through the front rooms and declaring them "just the same." Eleanor stepped out of the car and noticed with dismay that all her spring bulbs were half-dead with drought.

She opened the back door of her dark blue sedan and picked up the cat carrier. Jasmine opened one resentful green eye and closed it again. She was undoubtedly car sick, but too proud to vomit on her lovely white fur. Eleanor carried her over to the grass, then unlocked the carrier door. When Jasmine felt better she'd crawl out to explore her new surroundings.

Eleanor examined the outside of the house with trepidation, but to her relief found that not much had changed in two years. The roof showed no obvious signs of damaged shingles; the white clapboard siding was in remarkably good shape; the porch looked newly varnished, and even the shutters and porch railing were sparkling with dark green paint. *I bet Nathan did this*, she realized. Her gratitude almost made her cry, but she managed to control herself so she could show a good face to Peter, who was bounding back out of the cottage.

"C'mon, Mom, I'll help you unpack. Then can I go to the beach before supper?"

"Sure, go ahead."

She had no idea if that was the best thing to say. Ever since Bill had died, everything she did as a parent was fraught with confusion. Was it safe for a fourteen-year-old to go to the beach by himself? What if she needed him for something before he got back? What would Bill have answered? "Just be back by 6:00," she added.

As she watched her tanned son toss his blond head and lift three and four bags at a time onto his shoulders, she wished once again that he didn't seem like a stranger to her. How was he able to be so carefree? He had grieved, he had accepted, he was growing up. And she was standing still, stuck in a time-warp of loss. Everything she did, every decision made, was done in a muck of uncertainty and sadness. Most days she barely had the strength to get up in the morning.

She pulled the remaining bags from the trunk and carried them into the house.

Peter was busy in the kitchen, unpacking food and sundries, laying them out on the counter for her to put away. He carefully folded the paper bags - reserving one to place in the plastic garbage can - and put them in their old spot in the crack between the two lower cabinets. Finishing that, he grabbed his two suitcases from the hallway and raced upstairs. Eleanor listened to the sound of opening and shutting drawers as he quickly put a summer's worth of clothing away. She heard him hopping around as he pulled up his swim trunks, then he bounced downstairs, opened another suitcase to grab a beach towel, called out good-bye, and was out the door. An instant silence replaced him.

It was frightfully hot in the kitchen. Eleanor was pleased with herself for remembering to call Nathan in advance to turn on the generator - at least the fruits and vegetables wouldn't wilt in the refrigerator. But what to do about the rest of the house? None of the fans would do any good unless she opened the windows, and there were too many bees and mosquitoes to risk that without putting in the screens. She thought of the number of windows in the cottage and the great number of screens she would have to install, and felt thoroughly incapable. But that wouldn't do - they'd suffocate tonight in the house unless she took care of it.

"Okay, you can do this," she told herself. Where would Bill have kept the screens? Maybe the garage out back; no, more likely the attic. Eleanor had only been up there a few times, but she remembered vaguely that Bill used to run in and out of there at the beginning and end of every summer. She climbed the stairs to the second floor and looked around. *How did one get up there, anyway?* Then she remembered the linen closet had a half-door that opened to reveal the hidden stairs. Finding the door, she ducked down and climbed up.

It was stifling hot in the attic, but right away she saw the screens, stacked neatly under the window, behind a huge walnut desk. It was an old-fashioned, monstrous thing with a top at least three feet deep. Still, she thought she could probably lean over it and pull up the screens.

She stretched her 5 foot 4 inch frame over the desk as far as she could. She could just grab the screens, but try as she might she couldn't get the leverage to lift them. *Damn*, she thought, *I'll have to move the desk.*

The desk, however, refused to budge. She pulled, and pushed, and prodded, and cursed, until sweat ran down her face in streams, and finally, completely frustrated, she burst into tears and kicked the bottom of the desk with all her might.

The bottom of the lower left drawer fell out. "Oh, great!" she exclaimed, beside herself with anger. A part of her wanted to lose control - throw things, scream out loud, have a complete hysterical fit - but the voice of Reason, the voice that had maintained her sanity for two years, said sternly, "Cut it out. You're acting like a child." Instantly she sobered. She knew only too well that Reason was her lifeline, and must be obeyed at all costs.

She dried her tears and felt calmer. Bending down, she tried to lift the drawer back into place, and as she did so she noticed something sitting on the drawer bottom. It looked like a stack of papers.

4

Carefully she tried to pull it out, under the desk, but the space wasn't large enough. So very gingerly she re-lifted the bottom back into place, and tried to open the drawer. To her surprise, it pulled out smoothly.

The white thing was indeed a stack of papers - a bundle of letters. Tied neatly with a faded green ribbon, there appeared to be quite a number of them. Curious, Eleanor untied the ribbon and picked up the letter on top. It was addressed to "Lizzie Johnson" in Waltham, Massachusetts. Eleanor couldn't remember Bill or anyone in his family having the name Johnson. But the letter appeared quite old, so maybe it was an ancient relative. The cottage had been in Bill's family for a long time.

Eleanor opened the letter and read:

January 13, 1903

Dear Lizzie,

Ever since Will died, my life has been meaningless.

Eleanor gasped and dropped the letter as if it had burned her fingers. A strange chill ran up her spine and she shivered, despite the temperature in the attic. *Who was Will, a name so similar to Bill, and why did the letter have to do with death?* Glancing suspiciously at the fallen paper, she hastily re-folded it and stuffed it back into its envelope, setting it back on top of the pile.

In a moment, she felt very silly. It was a ridiculous reaction - how could a letter from almost one-hundred years ago have anything to do with her?

She looked again at the bundle of letters. Curiosity overwhelmed her superstitions. She thought to herself that perhaps if she started at the *bottom* of the pile, she would begin with earlier letters, and build up to the death part.

She picked up the letters, turned the pile upside down, and tentatively opened the first letter. She just had time to feel relief that her guess was correct - the letter was dated 1883 - when a pounding on the front door downstairs caught her ear.

She hastily returned the letter to its sleeve, grabbed the whole packet and the ribbon, and yelled, "Coming!" as loudly as she could. She hurried down the attic stairs, crouched out through the half-door, and was about to descend the main staircase when something made her pause.

"Just a minute!" she called, and running to her bedroom, she threw the letters on her bed and shut the door. Then she hastened down to answer the knocking.

It was Nathan. "Hi, Ellie, I just stopped by to welcome you back."

No one in Boston called her Ellie; she was Eleanor to all her school friends. But Bill had called her Ellie, and introduced her to everyone in Annisquam that way, so every summer, "Ellie" she became.

"Nathan, it's so good to see you! Please come in."

As Nathan stepped into the house, Eleanor thought that he hadn't changed much. His dark red waves were perhaps receding a little, but he still had his baby face - the kind that showed you how he'd looked at age three and at age fifteen. Yet you couldn't mistake his body for anything but a grown man's - lean and muscular, and lightly freckled from all his outdoor work.

"Nathan, you painted and varnished, didn't you? The cottage looks great! I expected all kinds of weather damage - it was really very kind of you."

"No problem. You know I like to look out for these old cottages."

"I'm glad you're here. I'm trying to get the window screens out of the attic, but they're stuck behind a big desk. Would you mind helping me? It's absolutely broiling in here."

"Sure. Show me the way."

As they climbed upstairs, Nathan told her that everyone in town had missed them last year. "If the heat breaks," he added, "the ladies will be around to see you tomorrow. They've been asking me everyday if I knew when you were arriving."

By "the ladies," Eleanor knew he meant the older women who had lived in Annisquam their whole lives - Grace Pippin, Miranda Cowling, maybe Lydia Meyerhoff. They had known Bill's parents and watched Bill grow up. Inwardly, Eleanor sighed. She loved those ladies, but she dreaded the first reunion. No one ever knew what to say to her, and she never knew how to react.

As if he read her mind, Nathan suddenly asked, "So how are you holding up, Ellie?"

"Oh, fine, I guess."

Nathan had actually come to the funeral - the official "Annisquam representative" - one of the only people from Bill's generation still living in the area. He was about five years younger than Bill, so they weren't best friends, but all the real 'Squam kids had played together as children, as relatively few families lived there year round. As adults, he and Bill had had even more in common - they both had university careers. Bill had taught English at Harvard; Nathan taught architecture at MIT - and put up with the commute to Cambridge, so he could live all year in Annisquam.

"See how they're stuck?" They had reached the attic and Eleanor pointed out the screens. Easily, Nathan reached over the desk and lifted them up. A six-foot frame came in handy sometimes.

"Thanks. That was impossible for me."

"Would you like some help putting them in?"

Eleanor hesitated. She very much wanted help, but felt obligated to do it herself. She couldn't rely on other peoples' help all the time. "Maybe you could show me how to do it, and I'll take it from there."

"Ellie, it's two hundred degrees in this house. I'll show you, but then let me do some of them. Two can do the job a lot faster than one."

"Well, all right. If it's no trouble."

Nathan worked the first floor, and Eleanor said she'd do the second floor. She felt self-conscious about the letters on her bed. For some reason, she wanted them to remain her secret.

In short time, the screens were in and the fans were on, and the house felt less like an oven. They poured themselves glasses of ice water, and sat out on the front steps. Jasmine, fully recovered, entertained them by stalking a butterfly through the grass.

Peter came up the hill from the beach right on time. At the first glance of Nathan, he broke into a huge grin and ran up to greet him. Nathan tousled his hair and the two of them began an animated conversation about the changes in town.

Eleanor was amazed. Two years ago, Peter had been a shy twelve-year-old who rarely spoke to adults unless spoken to. Now here he was, jabbering away like he and Nathan were old friends. It pleased her immensely to just sit quietly and listen to him.

But after a few minutes, she felt the cheerfulness drain out of her, and a familiar sense of exhaustion and sadness took its place. It was like a cloud that hung over her, blocking the sunshine, whenever she began to feel a bit happy. She didn't believe it was right to be happy.

She heard Nathan break off his conversation and remark, "Peter, I think your Mother's tired. Maybe I'd better get going."

The joy left Peter's face too, and Eleanor felt a twinge of guilt. "Okay. But I'll see you tomorrow, right?"

"Right. Meet me at Mrs. Conboy's house at 10:00 am."

"Okay!"

Eleanor rose as Nathan prepared to leave. "Bye," she said, "thanks again for your help." Nathan waved away the thanks, and Peter and Eleanor watched him walk down the street.

Peter turned to his mother. "Mom, isn't that great about the summer job?"

"What summer job?"

"Weren't you listening? Nathan's gonna let me help him paint this summer. We're starting with Mrs. Conboy's old house."

"That's great, honey. I'm sorry, I guess I was thinking of something else."

Peter looked at her for a moment, as if there was something he wanted to say. But he seemed to think better of it, picked up his towel and headed indoors.

* * * *

Dinner that night was hastily thrown together - salad and coldcuts - it was still far too hot to consider turning on the stove. Eleanor and Peter ate in relative silence, as had become their way. Eleanor was always preoccupied - worrying about things she had to take care of. After a polite question or two about his afternoon at the beach, Eleanor's conversation dissolved. Peter ate quickly, cleared the dishes, and disappeared into his room.

After a while, the "thump, thump" of muzzled base told Eleanor that Peter had turned on his portable CD player. The sound roused her from the kitchen table, and she remembered the letters on her bed.

Sneaking upstairs so Peter wouldn't notice her, she slipped into her room and closed the door. She flopped down on the bed and pulled over the oldest letter.

It was again addressed to "Lizzie Johnson" in Waltham, same street address. The handwriting was the same too. She looked at the return address: "Pleasure Point, Annisquam." Eleanor thought that was odd - there weren't any houses on the Point. Their cottage was on Planter's Neck.

The paper was brittle, so Eleanor was very careful unfolding it. The handwriting was scrawling, but feminine, and easy to read. There were two full sheets. It began:

June 30, 1883

Dear Lizzie,

You would not believe all the fun you are missing! Cousin Charles and I have organized a baseball game on the beach. We play everyday at four. Frank is the bat boy, and even Ida has condescended to watch us though she thinks I am silly for playing a <u>boy's</u> game. Ad Butler is our umpire and Mama brings lemonade. <u>Everyone</u> plays - Oscar Perkins, Walter Adams, Fred Pousland, Doc Emerson and Mr. Harraden, the Babson brothers, and, well everyone - even Captain Davis played once! I've had ten base hits in four games so no one dares to tease me, and the ladies cheer more for me than anyone. I can't wait for you to see!

Ida and Frank are angels except that they both torture me relentlessly. Ida always wants me to have tea parties with her dolls, which you know I detest, and Frank tries to drown me every time I dare to go in the water. They both miss their Mama, as I do! <u>When</u> are you coming? Surely the ladies at the Auxiliary can do without you for a while - you <u>need</u> a vacation to get rejuvenated for next year. I am going to write to William separately and demand that he bring you, as his husbandly duty.

Oh, Lizzie, you will never guess who has taken the twin. A famous artist and his family. Cousin Katherine knows them and has introduced us. William Lamb Picknell is the artist, and he's here with his mother, and two younger sisters, Nellie and Minnie (who are very nice, by the way), and his younger brother George, who's my age. George plays baseball with us, but his brother paints in the afternoon. Aunt Tot says he's just returned from

11

abroad and he's very famous - he painted a picture of a road in France that won an honor at the Paris Salon a few years ago. He shows at Williams & Everett's - we must go see sometime, ne c'est pas?

Eleanor paused in surprise. *I know that artist,* she realized, *he did that painting I love at the Museum of Fine Arts.* She had always been fascinated by the huge canvas, "Morning on the Loing." *How strange that he should have something to do with these people. I wonder what the "twin" is?* she pondered, but couldn't figure it out, and continued reading:

Now, Lizzie, the next part is to you in confidence, so if you are reading this out loud to anyone please skip to the next section. I need my older (and wiser) sister's advice. I have been feeling very strange since we got here, Lizzie, as if there are butterflies in my stomach all the time. It's as if something important is about to happen to me, but I don't know what! It makes me giddy half the time, and miserable the rest. I keep getting out of sorts with Mama, which you know is not like me, and I am so restless when we go calling. I want to be outdoors all the time, and alone, but then I get lonely. What is wrong with me, Lizzie? Did you ever feel anything like this?

Mama says it is "resistance to growing up." Or, rather, she thinks I should behave like a lady all the time, and sew, and visit, and act demure, and certainly not play baseball. Only I don't feel like a lady yet. Should I? I __am__ nineteen. Most of my girlfriends have had beaux, as you know. But I don't want to get married. I don't know if I'll ever care to.

Well, this is a lot of questions, which I can see you won't be able to answer in a letter. So you must come soon!

But if not , write me something to cheer me up!

Love always,

Gertrude

P.S.   I hope you can remember back this far to when you were nineteen! (Only kidding!)

Well, thought Eleanor, *Gertrude is Lizzie's sister. Lizzie is married to William, and she is older, and it seems Ida and Frank are her children. But I wish I knew what any of them had to do with that old desk!*

Eleanor looked at the bundle of remaining letters, and started to reach for the next one.   But midway she stopped her hand.   She decided it was fun to have a mystery, and she didn't want to spoil it by reading all the letters at once.   And there was another reason, she admitted to herself.   She was afraid of the last letter.

I'll only read one a day, she promised. *That way I'll drag out the ending as long as possible.*

She lay back on the bed and read the first letter over again.   The phrase "resistance to growing up" stuck in her mind.   It reminded her of something.   She thought back to her own teenage years but, no, that wasn't it.   She couldn't wait to grow up when she was a teenager - she had always tried to act and behave older. She'd even preferred older friends; in fact, part of her attraction to Bill was that he was older.

She remembered how mature she'd tried to act when she'd met him, so he wouldn't think their 8-year difference was any obstacle.   She smiled, remembering how nervous she'd been when he'd actually asked her out!

Bill... resistance to growing up. Oh, yes, it was something *he'd* said to her, about that old truck in the garage. They'd argued because she didn't want to learn to drive a stick shift, and he'd insisted that it was important. If anything ever happened to him, he'd said, she'd need to know how to drive it. She'd answered that if anything every happened to him, she'd just get rid of it. And Bill had lost his patience, and accused her of not wanting to be a real adult, of not wanting to be able to take care of herself. She'd been very uncomfortable with that argument. *Well, I hope you're satisfied now*, she thought angrily. *Something did happen to you.* Eleanor felt bitter tears well up in her eyes. "Why did you leave me? Why? I hate you for leaving me!" she whispered into the air. She sobbed into her pillow, not because she was angry, but because she felt so guilty about being angry. "I wish I could just go away and be left alone," she cried to him, beyond the grave. But as always, there was no one to answer her.

Eventually she spent her tears, got up to wash her face, and went to bed, exhausted.

2

The next day dawned much cooler, so much so
that Eleanor turned off the fans. Clouds were dark on
the horizon, and the breeze was up, but she couldn't
tell if the storm would stay out to sea or move towards
shore. Eleanor felt a pang of longing. Bill had always
been good at predicting the weather. Sometimes she
missed him so much she physically ached.

She was awake quite early, as she often was.
Something would startle her in her sleep, and she'd
wake up to find that it was impossible to fall back
asleep, because her mind raced with unhappy thoughts.
She hated those hours of loneliness before the rest of
the world awoke. She made coffee for herself, enticed
the cat inside to eat, and thought, watching her nibble,
how lucky Jasmine was to have someone to see to her
every need. When Jasmine began washing her paws,
Eleanor picked her up. She held her in her lap,
stroking her and murmuring, "I wish you could take
care of me for a change," an indignity that Jasmine,
much to her credit, put up with. Eleanor held her until
Jasmine relaxed and purred, and then, satisfied that the
cat, at least, still loved her, she gently put her down.

Well, if "the ladies" were really coming today,
she'd need something to serve. She could bake -

goodness, she couldn't even remember the last time she had, but then, she couldn't remember the last time she'd had an occasion that warranted it. For months after Bill's death, she'd still had baked goods in the freezer from well-meaning friends. They couldn't have known that she could not eat any of it. To look at it only reminded her of her loss; to eat it was like eating dust and ashes. But today, for some reason, the thought of an old favorite recipe - a lemon & poppy seed cake - sounded comforting. She'd have to go to the store for the ingredients.

Now was as good a time as any. She climbed back upstairs to take a quick shower, and there, on her bureau, she spied the packet of letters. *It's awfully early*, she thought. *If I read one now that's it for the day.* Nevertheless, the desire was unstoppable - she picked up the next letter.

It was dated August 25, 1883. Same year, same addresses, same handwriting. Eleanor suspected that all the letters were from Gertrude to Lizzie, but she didn't want to peek to find out.

Dear Lizzie,

It seems as if the season is quieting down. Many of the summer guests are leaving - the Halls left yesterday - and without your family, Mama and I find the cottage spacious, and a bit lonely. I almost wish we'd left with you, except for my afternoons with Nellie Picknell. It was so nice of her to invite me to learn watercolors with her. I do so enjoy sitting on the beach at the end of the day, painting and talking. Of course my work is atrocious, but talent seems to run in her family, as hers is quite handsome. We are both painting the lighthouse with a sunset behind it, although you would never know our pictures were meant for the same scene, for every time I work on the sky my colors run into the building!

Sometimes Minnie joins us. She wants to be a newspaper correspondent and she brings her pad along and practices making observations. They are all very studious, aren't they? Except George, who is a clown. He only comes by to tease us.

Last evening Mama and I were invited to come by after supper, and William was home. He showed us his large landscape, and his fisherman. Both are wonderful! I've never seen anything like them for truthfulness - you can feel the heat on the shoulders of his lobsterman, while the landscape is cooler, with clouds coming in from the east. I admire him so much! I intend to educate myself at the Art Museum this year, so I can speak to him of his work with some intelligence.

Nellie has told me some very interesting things about her brother, and as they are of a personal nature I would be loathe to repeat them, except to you, dear Lizzie, because you are the soul of discretion. I know you will not spread rumors. Nellie says that William is in love with an English general's daughter, and that they are half-afraid he will marry abroad and never come home again. He is going back to England this winter to be near her family, and the worst of it is - Nellie has met her and <u>does</u> <u>not</u> <u>like</u> <u>her</u>. She thinks she puts on airs, and thinks herself better than the rest of them, although she is always perfectly polite. I suggested that perhaps she was shy and it was just her way. Nellie expressed surprise at me, because that is exactly what William told her! Still, she has her doubts, her "intuition" tells her the girl will not make her brother happy, and she frets about it, as they are very close, as you know.

Lizzie, I do feel so much happier than I did at the beginning of the summer, just as you said I would. But I can't help but feel it is at least partly owing to my new friendships. I find Nellie and Minnie's company soothing. They are so kind to me, and never treat me like a child, and yet they don't bore me with silly love affairs and empty-headed flirtations. They are very <u>serious</u>-minded girls, with real careers and aspirations. You saw Nellie's published poetry - she is an excellent writer. They are fine companions and examples, and don't make me feel naive because I have not experienced any affaires de coeur.

Mama says to tell you we have fixed the date for departure - September 15. We will telegram with the time of the train. You may tell Ida that I will drill her mercilessly on her spelling when I return. Tell Frank that I found another fine shell for his collection, and that I expect him to mind his Mama until I am home, and then he can misbehave with me.

Love to both of them, and to my dear brother-in-law, whose baseball feats are still touted by all the 'Squamers. Mama sends kisses.

Much love,

Gertrude

Eleanor thought it was a very pleasing letter, and was glad Gertrude was feeling more composed. She liked things and people to be composed - at least lately she did - because chaos meant things were not controllable. She wanted no more to do with uncontrollable circumstances.

Eleanor started the shower and thought about Nellie and Minnie Picknell, poet and journalist. She remembered how serious she had once been about her own writing, before she was married. In fact, it was because of her writing that she'd met Bill. After her senior year in college, she'd taken a summer course at Harvard for graduate credit, a writing seminar led by renowned novelist William Strayer.

Eleanor had never heard of William Strayer, author of <u>The Snowy Desert</u> and <u>The Road to Willowbank</u>, but one look at his sandy brown curls and denim-blue eyes and she knew he was God's gift to writing. Although she would spend her hours in the seminar in a daze of blushing adoration, she attacked her homework assignments with a fierce determination to write *well.* Her hard work paid off - by the end of the summer she had won his respect, and, as she had also intended, been noticed for her attractions as a pretty, single woman. After the closing bell of the last class he asked her out.

She remembered the moment perfectly. They'd been standing on the steps of Sever Hall, as a group, writers who had bonded and hated to say good-bye. Slowly the other seminar students had drifted away; she had a sense, an intuition, that Bill wanted her to stay. Finally only the two of them were left. They began walking across campus - it was a ripe summer day and everything was deep green. A gentle breeze relieved the heat and the sky was an azure color she couldn't remember ever having seen before. He stopped on the path and turned towards her, grinning with sudden shyness. "Would you like to go to dinner sometime?" he had asked. It was the right choice. If he had asked her for coffee she wouldn't have known if it was a date, or just an extension of the casual friendliness of the class. She blurted out "Yes" before he'd half-finished the question, destroying forever any chance she might have had at appearing worldly and experienced. Oh, well, she was only twenty-two, and the idol of her life had just granted her heart's desire.

Looking back, it was hard to believe the relationship had ever progressed. She'd been so nervous the first few dates, that she barely ate and would become suddenly silent with painful self-consciousness. Slowly, however, Bill metamorphosed from her idolized professor to a real human being. Soon she began to see how he was outside of class - at home, on a road trip, or at the beach house, here, with his parents - and he became a complete person with many facets, and many attributes beyond his looks and his talent. When she really began to know him, she opened up.

Still, throughout their relationship, a part of Eleanor never stopped idolizing him. In her eyes, he was always wise, always strong, always confident. She measured herself against his perceived perfection, and became aware of how often she fell short.

As she stepped out of the shower a strange feeling overcame Eleanor, a darkness shadowed her happy reminiscences. For a brief moment she felt resentment. Something had been lost of herself, in her love for Bill. She didn't like the thought - she pushed it away, and angrily pulled on her clothes, chiding herself for once again ruining perfectly good memories. Then she sighed and thought that everything was ruined now. Bill's death had upset everything she took for granted, even her memories.

The phone rang downstairs in the kitchen and to her surprise she heard Peter answer it. He must have gotten up while she was in the shower. After a few moments he was calling, "Mom!"

"Who is it?"

"It's Grandma Mary!" Bill's mother. Ever since Bill's death it had been both painful and comforting to talk to her. Mary always maintained a cheerful outlook, perhaps just for Eleanor's sake. Eleanor was sophisticated enough to understand that on one level this was unfair to Mary - Mary had her own grief and shouldn't have to ease Eleanor's pain - but then it was also good for Mary to still be needed by a younger person. And Eleanor did need her, although she also resented needing her, and would always hate herself afterwards when a conversation with Mary resulted in nostalgic tears. It was all so complicated!

Eleanor ran downstairs to pick up the phone. "Mom? Hi. How's Dad?" Mary and Ben were her closest family. Eleanor's father had passed away years ago, and her mother, at age seventy-five, was in a nursing home in Boston, and was fairly "out of it." Eleanor had been a late baby, or an "accident" as her older brothers had affectionately teased, and Eleanor was rarely in touch with these two siblings who were ten and twelve years her senior.

"He's fine, dear. He's off on the golf course as usual." Bill's parents had retired to Pompano Beach, Florida eight years ago. That's when Bill and Eleanor had inherited the cottage, although they had spent most of their summers in Annisquam with Bill's parents before that. "How's the weather in Annisquam?" Mary asked.

"Yesterday was broiling. Today it looks like it might rain."

"It won't," Peter announced with authority, from the kitchen table.

21

"Oh, Peter says it won't. He's sitting here eating breakfast."

"Well, Peter learned weather from Bill, so I'm sure he's right. How's the house?"

"It's in beautiful shape. Nathan painted it, would you believe. Wasn't that nice? He helped me put the screens in yesterday, too. And he's given Peter a summer job - Peter's going to help him paint."

"Nathan's always been fond of you, Ellie."

Eleanor instinctively brushed the comment aside. She found it disturbing, especially coming from Bill's mother. "Well, I don't know what this town would do without him."

That was true. Nathan took care of all the old-timers' homes. Every summer he picked out a few to paint and repair, at no charge. He claimed it was done purely out of love of architectural history, that he hated to see the old cottages deteriorate. But everyone knew Nathan also loved the residents themselves; he loved listening to their stories of old Annisquam, and enjoyed easing, just a little, their old-age worries. Nathan was one in a million, and everybody loved him.

"So, how are you getting along?" Mary asked.

"Fine, so far. I think it was a good idea to come. Peter's happy. And one place is as good as the next for me."

"Oh, Ellie, don't talk that way. I was hoping that getting out of Boston might help you feel better. I've always found the beach comforting."

"Well, then that's my problem. I haven't been down to the beach yet."

"Now, Ellie, don't joke."

"Sorry." She paused, then added hesitantly,

22

"There are a lot of memories here."

"I know. Good memories can be painful, but they help us heal."

"I guess so." She hadn't said the memories were good, Mary just assumed so. But then, why shouldn't she? Eleanor always had been happy in Annisquam. That was what made it so bittersweet now. "I'm trying, Mom, really. Oh, Grace and Miranda are coming today!"

"How nice! Give them my love."

"I will. Oh, Mom, by the way, have you ever heard of a Lizzie Johnson?"

"No. Why do you ask?"

"Oh, it's nothing. Never mind. Listen, I've got to get to the store before the ladies arrive. I'll call you next week."

"Okay. Kiss Peter for me."

"Will do. Bye." Eleanor hung up the phone and turned to Peter. "Gram sends her love." She felt too awkward with him to go over and give him the kiss. "I'm going to the grocery store. Want to come?"

"I can't. I've got to meet Nathan."

"Oh, right." Eleanor realized she envied his having something specific to do everyday. He would be busy all summer, too busy to think. "Well, I'll see you at dinner then. Six o'clock."

"Okay."

Eleanor picked up her handbag and keys. Suddenly she felt inadequate again as a parent. Surely your child's first job deserved some words of encouragement or advice. "Peter, be careful when you're painting. On the ladder, I mean. And watch out for hornets' nests under the eaves."

Peter laughed at her. "I'll be careful," he assured

her with a mock groan, but then added, "Hey, that's a good idea about the hornets. I wouldn't have thought of that."

Eleanor felt good. It was the first time in two years she actually knew something her fourteen-year-old didn't. She left the house with a smile on her face.

*   *   *   *

When Peter arrived at the old Conboy house, he was surprised to find Nathan waiting for him with a few tools, but no paint. Nathan explained that they would have to scrape, caulk and prime the wood before they could begin painting. That was fine with Peter. Everything sounded like fun to him because it was all new, and because he'd be doing it with Nathan.

Peter was one of those rare individuals who intuitively know what they need to do to be happy. The loss of his father had been a tragedy; but to Peter, every bad blow that life dealt was simply a new challenge - identify the problem and find the best solution. His problem was that he missed his father, missed having an adult male around to guide him. The solution was to find a substitute. Peter decided he had one in Nathan.

Peter's attitude towards life was very much like his father's, although he was perhaps unaware of this fact. He had absorbed his father's credo: self-pity is not productive. This didn't mean he hadn't grieved, or wasn't still quietly grieving, it simply meant that he accepted sadness as a part of the fabric of life, not the meaning of it. There was a point to life and that was to get on with it. This was so obvious to him that he found his mother's attitude not only disturbing, but discouraging. He wanted to respect her, like before, but he wondered at her refusal to get over the death. That was how he saw it - refusal, not inability.

Peter understood that his mother would never be happy again unless she wanted to. But it was beyond Peter's constitution to fathom not wanting to be happy. To Peter, happiness was the point of existence. Suffering was a roadblock life threw in your way; if you wanted to lead a meaningful life, you had to learn to get around it. Peter found his mother incomprehensible, and was torn between love for her and despair at her weakness.

Nathan handed Peter a scraper and together they started in on the porch railing, which was peeling badly. After a while, Mrs. Conboy came out with large glasses of lemonade, which they happily gulped down, and carrot cake which they declined for the present. Cream cheese frosting was too sticky to eat while working outside on a warm day.

Nathan had a radio tuned in to one of the light rock stations, so they hummed and bopped a bit while they worked, happily companionable. At noon, Nathan brought out two salami and cheese sandwiches, potato chips, and sodas from his cooler. As they ate, they talked about their work, then their various experiences at school, and finally the inevitable subject - life without Bill.

"How's your mother doing, Peter?"

Peter paused for a moment before answering. He wasn't inclined to lie to Nathan with a casual "Oh, fine;" but he wasn't sure he was comfortable telling the truth. Finally he decided to be honest. Maybe Nathan could give him some advice.

"She's pretty messed up still. She cries a lot. I don't think she's really gotten over it."

Nathan was taken aback by the answer. He could tell from Peter's hesitation that it was at least as bad as he said it was. This was a surprise. Since the funeral two years ago, he'd assumed she'd been coping better every day. When he'd seen her yesterday she had seemed pretty good - a bit solemn perhaps, but not distraught. He realized that he really didn't know much about her at all.

"Does she have friends to talk to?" he asked.

"Well, she does, but it seems like she doesn't want to talk to them. They called a lot at the beginning, but she never wanted to see anyone. Now they mostly leave her alone. She doesn't like to discuss it - Dad's death I mean."

"That's not good. Talk is good for healing. Maybe she doesn't want to cry in front of her friends."

"Oh, she cries easily enough. I think she's angry."

"At who?"

"God...Fate...the universe. Dad...Me... I don't know, everybody!"

"Well, she could be angry. It's a common response to death."

"Yeah, but it's been a long time. And does she have to be angry with me?" Peter asked with passion. "I want to be her friend, but she won't talk to me anymore."

Nathan was impressed with the idea of a fourteen-year-old wanting to be a friend to his mother. Well, at least he could be a friend to the boy, try to fill a void. He felt now that his instinct to hire Peter for the summer had been on target. The boy needed another adult in his life. "Hang in there," he advised. "Give her time." Yet they both suspected that Eleanor needed more than time.

"Has your Mom seen any doctors or therapists since your Dad's death?" Nathan asked after a while. "Sometimes people need professional help to get over a big trauma."

"One of her friends gave her the phone number of a psychologist who specializes in grief therapy. But I heard her tell another friend that she didn't want to go. The phone number sat on a piece of paper by the phone for ages, then a few months ago I saw her throw it away. I don't think she ever called him."

Nathan wondered why, if Eleanor was so unhappy, she didn't want help. Even in the stodgiest New England circles, therapy was totally accepted. She couldn't be worried about a "stigma" - so what was she trying to avoid?

All this new information about Eleanor was disturbing. Nathan had had a mild crush on her for fifteen years - since the first time he'd met her. It was nothing serious - he completely respected the fact that she was Bill's - but all these years hers had been the standard by which he judged all the other women he'd met. He saw her now as she'd been all those years ago: petite, energetic and beautiful, with a bright smile and flashing green eyes that complimented her dark auburn hair. Undoubtedly his vision of her had been rosy and embellished, and now he was seeing how little he really knew about her. Strangely, as it made her more human, it took away his intimidation. He felt warmly towards her, worried about her, a bit protective. She might not be perfection anymore, but as a real person she was infinitely more interesting. Nathan began to replace his secret fantasy of a summer of admiring her from afar, with one of becoming a real friend. Knowing how upset she still was about Bill's death, he would have been ashamed to think of that friendship leading to anything else.

Peter interrupted his reverie. "Do you think maybe spending the summer here will cheer her up? I heard her tell Grandma this morning that there were a lot of memories here. I don't know if that's good or bad."

"We'll have to see. The people of this town love her, and you. They don't always take to newcomers that quickly, but your Dad's family has been here so long that everyone was interested in who your Dad would marry. When it turned out to be someone as pretty, and friendly, and generous as your mother, they couldn't help but like her. They bark a mean bite, but 'Squam natives are very good people when you come right down to it. So they'll be reaching out to her; it all depends on whether she'll let them in."

Peter chewed some potato chips for a moment, before speaking again. "Hearing you talk about her like that, really brings back the old days. She's like a different person. Before and after. I hope the real Mom is still in there somewhere."

"I hope so too," Nathan agreed, and added to himself, *for your sake, Peter.*

* * * *

There was a knock on the door promptly at 3:00 p.m. Three was the optimum time for afternoon tea - too late to interfere with lunch, too early to ruin anyone's dinner plans. The Annisquam ladies were scions of etiquette.

Miranda Cowling held a plate of her homemade chocolates in her hand, while Grace Pippin held a bouquet of peonies from her renowned garden. Both were wearing flowered dresses and hats, and looked sweet as butter. Slightly behind them stood Lydia Meyerhoff, awkwardly shoving her keys into her purse and smoothing down her suit. Lydia was the former schoolteacher, and she still retained a "let's get down to business" attitude that had frightened generations of youngsters on their first day of school. She was tall, and although well into her sixties, still tanned, trim and athletic. Miranda and Grace were older, more petite, and exuded warmth and cheerfulness. Grace was probably close to eighty, but she remembered everything as if it had happened yesterday. Eleanor noticed that she walked stiffly now, but Miranda was still as sprite as an elf.

"Oh, come in! It's so nice to see you!"

"We wanted to surprise you," Grace began, "but that young Nathan spilled the beans, I hear."

"Well, it's just as well, because you might not have caught me in," Eleanor said. Of course, this was technically a lie - Eleanor knew she never had any plans - but it seemed like a nice thing to say, for Nathan's sake.

Eleanor directed the ladies to the parlor, where she had already set out the poppy-seed cake, and tea cups. She added the plate of chocolates to the table, then announced, "Let me take these flowers into the kitchen and put them in water. Then I'll bring in some tea."

As she was leaving, Eleanor heard Lydia mutter with satisfaction: "Well, the house looks fine. Doesn't look like she'll let it go to pot." Eleanor suppressed the urge to be hurt by the comment.

After the tea was poured it was necessary to ask all around how everyone was. Lydia talked about her work - she was still trying to identify and classify all of the waterfowl on Cape Ann, and was beginning to think she had them all. No one had reported spotting a new bird for at least six months now. This brought a comment from Miranda that she couldn't imagine for the life of her how Lydia could remain interested in birds for all these years, but Lydia simply pursed her lips together and did not deign to reply, since she was well aware that the town thought her eccentric.

Eleanor quickly brought the subject around to Miranda's children, who were the joy of her life, and listened with polite interest while Miranda expounded on the latest escapades of Thomas, Jane, and Kelly, and their respective spouses and ingenious children. All three families lived in other parts of Massachusetts, but each managed to spend at least a week in Annisquam each summer, and Eleanor promised to visit them when they were in town. Grace had been waiting impatiently for her turn to speak, and now began with relish:

"I'm afraid I have nothing new to tell you about little old me, but we all want to hear about you, dear. How are you holding up? It was a great shock to all of us, I can tell you, and we did feel bad that we couldn't come to the funeral. I asked the Reverend Hope to say

30

a special prayer for you, and we had a moment of silence, but of course our thoughts being with you is not the same as being there ourselves."

"Thank you, that was very sweet. I didn't know."

"Didn't Nathan tell you? I sent him with specific instructions," Grace continued. "He was to represent us all. I hope he at least told you that."

Eleanor smiled. "Yes, he was very good to come for all of you. I know how hard it is for you to get around now." And indeed, the elder ladies of Annisquam did not drive, and no longer having living husbands, they relied on others to take them out of town. Which didn't happen very often, owing to various medicines that had to be taken on time, pets that needed special care, important appointments that couldn't be broken, and responsibilities for which everyone in town depended on them. In short, it did seem as if the town could not get by without them, which was quite likely the reason for their long lives.

"What exactly happened, my dear?" Miranda piped up. "I never did hear."

"It was an aneurysm," Eleanor answered solemnly. "An aortic aneurysm. It was very sudden." To her dismay, tears formed in her eyes. Grace leaned over and patted her hand.

"There, there. Miranda and I have both lost our husbands. It's a very painful thing. No one expects you to get over it right away."

Eleanor smiled gratefully. "It's funny you should say that. It seems to me that everyone *does* expect me to get over it by now. I just don't know how."

"Bill was a wonderful man, and you loved him

very much. But time heals all wounds. You will get better," Miranda announced with remarkable sanguineness.

I don't want to, Eleanor thought stubbornly to herself. *I don't want to stop loving him.* She turned from Grace and Miranda and spoke to Lydia, who had been stirring her tea uncomfortably. Lydia had never married, and conversations about husbands made her feel awkward. Eleanor changed the subject.

"Lydia, have you ever heard of a Lizzie Johnson in Annisquam, years ago?"

"Why ask her? I'm the oldest," snapped Grace.

"I'm really asking all of you," laughed Eleanor. "I just thought Lydia might have come upon her name in her research." Lydia was not only interested in waterfowl, but also in everything else about Annisquam.

"No, I don't think so," Lydia replied. "Why do you ask?"

"Oh, I found some reference to her in the house." Eleanor fudged the truth again, still reluctant to reveal the letters' existence.

"What kind of reference?" asked Grace, who never missed a trick.

Eleanor sighed inwardly and gave up. "Some letters. A packet of them. From someone named Gertrude to a Lizzie Johnson, apparently her sister. They were written in the 1880s."

"Well, the best source for information of that sort is the Annisquam Historical Society," Miranda responded. "Lydia, when are they open? I know they are almost always closed."

"Monday afternoons and Thursday evenings," Lydia answered. "But call first. That way someone can pull out the information you need."

"Do they have a lot of information on past residents of town?" Eleanor asked.

"They might. If the person left their mark."

Eleanor wondered if Gertrude or Lizzie Johnson could possibly have "left their mark." However, surely the artist, William Lamb Picknell, must have. "I'll stop by later in the week," she announced. "Thank you for the tip, Miranda."

"This cake is delicious," Grace announced.

"Thank you. It's the first thing I've baked, since... since the funeral."

"Well, you haven't lost your touch," noted Miranda. It was a sweet compliment, as Miranda was considered the best cook in town.

"I'm afraid I have a long way to go before I'm as good as you," Eleanor replied graciously.

"Did I ever tell you that when Bill was a child, I once made the mistake of giving him a cookie when he brought me a note from his mother? For weeks afterward he showed up on my doorstep every afternoon expecting another one. I kept on giving them to him, but I wondered whether or not his mother knew he kept coming over. Well, one day Mary was visiting me, when up to the door comes Bill. 'Bill,' she asks him, 'what are you doing here?' And Bill answers her, very proudly, 'Mrs. Cowling likes to give me cookies.' Well, I just could have died, but it was so cute."

Eleanor smiled. "He never did stop liking cookies, especially yours."

"Well, I dare say he didn't show it. He grew up to cut quite a handsome figure, didn't he?"

"Yes," Eleanor replied wistfully.

A shadow of sadness fell over the tea party. For a young man to be cut down in his prime, a child they had all watched grow up...

"God works in mysterious ways," mumbled Lydia, absently, while Grace and Miranda silently contemplated the vagaries of death.

Eleanor looked at her companions and wondered if any of them had ever felt as she did, as completely lost. *Did they ever suffer so much, and then did they learn to be happy again?* she wondered. She wished she knew. She felt she might find comfort in knowing that these strong, virile women had once felt that they couldn't go on. But she couldn't ask. She thought it might be cruel to dredge up old wounds. Besides, in order to discuss it she would have to reveal too much about herself. "More tea?" she offered.

"Well, just a bit," Grace said. "Then we must be going. There's a library board meeting tonight."

"You ought to consider joining us," Miranda offered. "We could use some bright, young women."

"Thank you. I'll consider it." *The library board.* It sounded so stodgy, just like what a widow would join. Something to do when your life was basically over. *That's unfair*, she chided herself. *They are only trying to be nice.*

But Lydia chimed in, "Gracious! The library board! Surely she's got more interesting things to do than join a bunch of us old fogies! Never mind Miranda, Eleanor, she forgets that you're still much too young for library boards."

"Well, really, Lydia, I don't see that it's all that awful. We make important decisions," Miranda said petulantly.

"Stop you two. Lydia has a point, Miranda.

34

None of us joined the board before we were fifty."

Miranda relaxed into a chuckle. "You're right, Grace. So we were. But what about the sewing circle?"

"Give it up, Miranda. Let the girl find her own way," Lydia insisted.

Eleanor listened to the conversation with growing interest. It was fun to be discussed as if she wasn't there. *If only someone else <u>could</u> make all the decisions for me*, she thought. *Life would be so much easier.* "I don't know if I'm quite up to joining any clubs or boards right now," she said. "But when I am, I'll be sure to check in with Miranda."

Everyone laughed. The ladies rose. "It was a lovely afternoon," they said. "Give our love to Mary and Ben when you speak with them."

"I will."

"And stop by next week, after you've been to the Historical Society," Grace added. "I'd like to hear more about that."

Eleanor was surprised. Grace seemed to have noticed that the subject meant something more to her than idle interest. "I will," Eleanor found herself promising.

After the ladies left, Eleanor slowly cleaned up the cake plates and tea cups. Crumbs and tea stains. It seemed a fitting metaphor for what was left of a person after they were gone. Gone down the street, or gone to heaven. Eleanor suddenly felt very tired. *Why does everything have to seem so sad to me? Why? I think I would give anything to feel hopeful again.*

Outside a sea gull let out a sudden cry. It roused Eleanor, and she shook off her misery. *Peter will be home soon. I'd better see about dinner.* She thanked God for the motions of life, for they were often the only things that kept her going.

It was raining the next morning, and Nathan telephoned to say that he and Peter would not be working. Eleanor was faced with the prospect of a whole day alone with her son. She had dreaded days like this in Boston, although they had been rare. Peter had school, or his friends. But none of the boys Peter played with in Annisquam had arrived for the summer yet, so he wouldn't have anywhere else to go. Eleanor wished guiltily that she could hide in her room all day. Peter and she would have nothing to say to each other, and the pain of that was more than she wanted to face.

Well, after breakfast I'll look around the house for a book. Maybe I can read all day. Get lost in someone else's story, she thought.

To her surprise, however, Peter suggested that the two of them play backgammon. He had located the old playing board and set it up on the back porch. The porch, a modern addition in historical terms - added on to the house in the 1960s - was screened in, so they could watch the rain without getting wet.

Eleanor found herself complying although she did not really feel like playing a board game. As she settled in to one of the rattan chairs, she noted that the cushions smelled slightly of mildew. *I'll have to see about that*, she realized, hoping they were not ruined for good. Every household incident that required action made her feel incapable and lonely. *Will I have to take care of everything, for the rest of my life, all by myself?*

They started playing, and Eleanor found herself enjoying it. It was nice to concentrate on something, to have an obvious topic of conversation. She was wrapped up in playing and commenting on the game, unaware that Peter had grown rather silent, in prelude to a conversation he was determined to have.

"Mom," he said, seemingly out of the blue, "what do you plan to do with your life?"

The question was so startling to Eleanor that she simply stared at him in response. She didn't have the slightest idea how to answer. She had no plans - why should she? What in the world were her options besides simply living day-to-day and hoping to feel better about it?

"I don't know what you mean," she said, stalling for time, and trying to get a better idea of what Peter might expect her to say. She was quite willing to say whatever would appease him, but she didn't know what that could possibly be.

"I mean, you've been dragging around for over two years now. You need a life. Friends. Something to do. Maybe you should see a doctor..." he added, shyly.

"I don't need a doctor," Eleanor snapped. "I don't know why everyone thinks it should be so easy for me to get over losing my husband. We had a life together, we had plans, everything was tied up in him... I can't just come up with a whole new life for myself just like that!" She snapped her fingers. "I need time!"

38

"Mom, I think you've had lots of time. Not to get over it - of course it still hurts. It hurts me too. But to get involved in things again. Do things. For two years you haven't even come to see me play ball, or come to a band concert."

Eleanor felt deflated. "So what you really mean is that I haven't been paying any attention to you! Oh, Peter, I'm so sorry."

"No, Mom!" To her surprise, he pounded his fist on the table. "It's not about me. It's about you. You're barely living! You just mope all the time. You need interests, friends. Don't you think it's time you snapped out of it?"

"Snapped out of it?" Eleanor was suddenly furious. "Obviously you think it's so easy. Well, maybe it is for you. But your father was my life, and I can't so easily forget him. Maybe you can, but I can't!"

Peter looked stunned, and his eyes filled with tears. *What have I done?* thought Eleanor. *What's wrong with me?* Peter got up from the table and blindly made his way to his room. Eleanor heard him slam the door, and she burst into tears.

For what seemed like an eternity, she sat there crying, her tears finally slowing to the pace of the drizzle outside. *Rain, sun, what's the difference? It's always a grey day.*

Strangely, the thought made her remember something. That was the name of a painting, by that artist, William Lamb Picknell. "A Grey Day." She had seen it once in a gallery window, one happy day long ago when she and Bill had gone window shopping up Newbury Street. The painting was a scene at the beach, storm clouds rolling in, the beach hard and grey under the looming dark sky. A few areas of dull green brush growing out of the sand. Yet the painting had been quiet, not sad. *I wonder why?* she asked herself. She felt there was an answer to the question, but it eluded her. She sighed. *I wonder if Gertrude ever saw him or his sisters again.*

Then she had a thought. Could the "Will" that dies be the artist? She was filled with a sense of premonition. *I just know he is.* She got up and went to the front of the house, where the parlor and living room had bookshelves. Ah, there it was. <u>Paintings in the Museum of Fine Arts</u>. William Lamb Picknell, 1853 to 1897. *Yes it could be him.*

But why would Gertrude be so devastated by his death? She barely knew him. A strange sense of fate came over Eleanor.

Unless...

She looked up the stairs. She wanted to get to the letters. For some reason, it was terribly important for her to know. Peter's door remained slammed shut; she could hear the base from his boom box. She could sneak past his door, he wouldn't know.

In the back of her mind a voice was telling her to go to her son, that she was a terrible mother, that she needed him more than she knew, that he needed her more than she knew. She ignored the voice. She wanted to read the letters. She climbed the stairs, passed Peter's room, entered her own and softly closed the door. Pulling the letters off her dresser, she determined to read as many as necessary to confirm what she suspected.

There was a gap of three years from the first two letters, but the addresses were still the same.

June 15, 1886

Dear Lizzie,

William is back this summer! He has come home from England! The marriage did not take place, and Nellie is so glad! I was afraid he would be sad and miserable, but he actually seems very happy to be here. Perhaps he did not love her all that much after all? I mentioned this to Nellie, but she just shook her head. She believes it was a tragic love affair, and William is just being brave.

He had much success in England. The Liverpool Gallery purchased his painting "Wintry March." And Nellie read me some reviews from the London papers - all the critics think very highly of him. You should see the work he is doing now. It is even better than two years ago. Remember when we went to see his painting in the Mechanic's Exhibition, the one that won the gold medal? I think his summer's work here will be even finer.

Annisquam is swarming with artists this summer. Robert Vonnoh is here, the Jones brothers, Mr. Joseph Decamp, a Mr. Frank Bicknell, cousin Katherine, of course, and the Hovendens. It is quite delightful to wander along the beach in the evening and see their day's work. Nellie and Minnie and I are becoming earnest critics - much to the dismay of many of the artists, who have no interest in our opinions. I think I am an embarrassment to Katherine! No, I am kidding, we keep our opinions only to ourselves, as we know we certainly couldn't do any better!

Lizzie, will you ask William to bring his camera

when you come? We could take a picture of all of the cottage residents together. I want to remember this summer! I am so happy!

I am counting the days until you arrive. Kiss Ida and Frank for me... I miss them!

Love,

Gertrude

The next letter was only ten days later.

June 25, 1886

Dear Lizzie,

I have scandalized the town again! I have learned to ride a safety bicycle. George Picknell brought his bicycle here for the summer, and Nellie, Minnie and I were completely intrigued. It looked like so much fun! I finally convinced George to let me try it, although I made him turn his back while I lifted my skirts to get on (which was not easy to do - why can't they ever take women's skirts into consideration when they design things?). Then he held on to the back and pushed me around town while I pedaled like crazy, yelling at him that under no circumstances was he to let go! After about fifteen minutes of this he was completely exhausted and told me flatly that if I wished to continue I was on my own. Nellie and Minnie looked very worried, but I said to George, "By golly, I'll do it myself!" and off I went, straight down Leonard Street until I lost control when a buggy turned on behind me and scared me half to death. I crashed, but all that skirt was good for something - it cushioned my fall! Everyone cheered and George helped me up and said I'd done very well for my first try, and I'm a little bruised but very proud of myself!

We are having so much fun this summer. William Picknell spends much more time with us than he used to. He has a new camera, and he takes pictures of the fishermen and then uses the images in his paintings. He says it is much easier than relying on perfect weather and water conditions. But, oh Lizzie, it is sometimes so funny to see, because he poses them in their boats on dry land, so that they really look ridiculous, but they are so serious about the whole thing that Nellie and Minnie and I just laugh and laugh! Then the fishermen laugh too and ruin the picture, and William gets mad at us, but not really as he is in fine spirits this year.

He and the Jones brothers - Hugh and Frank - are making a stained glass window out of shells they've collected on the beach. Every time any of us finds another pretty shell we bring it to them, so that now they have far too many for the project and are beginning to argue about which ones to use! It is to be a present for the Hovendens, and I think they will be delighted with it when it is finished.

Lizzie, this is the best summer ever. Hurry!

Love,

Gertrude

There was nothing more for that year. But there was a small flurry of letters from the end of the next year, again with the same addresses.

43

August 28, 1887

Dear Lizzie,

George and I went for a long walk today.
We started at the beach near the lighthouse, and ended up
in Rockport. We just kept going. I was feeling sad, and
the fresh air did me good.

They are all so nice to me. You know the feelings
of my heart, Lizzie. If you hadn't guessed last summer, I
would not have had the courage to confide in you. Thank
goodness it is only obvious to you! The others seem
oblivious. William doesn't notice me at all. I have no
talent in art or conversation to make him notice me, I
have no beauty to charm him. I wish I did not feel about
him so! Why do I not care for George? George likes me
very much, and I feel terrible that I only have eyes for his
brother. But George seems to know something. He told
me today while we were walking that his brother had no
time for love or marriage, that his career was everything
to him. Why did he tell me that? Is he trying to warn me,
or is he jealous and just wants me to forget about him?
Oh, listen to me, Lizzie - such a lot of balderdash! I am
just the friendly neighbor, comfortable Gertrude, no one
worth noticing.

Do you think Nellie and Minnie would still be
friends with me if they knew my feelings for their brother?
I hope so, I do not like to feel that I am deceiving them.
They are the best, truest friends anyone could wish for! I
know they would never deceive me. Am I bad, Lizzie?

You were so lucky, to have loved your William,
and him loving you, and you never went through these
tortures. Everyone knew you would get married, and you

44

did!

Oh, Lizzie, I would give anything to be happy again.

Love,

Gertrude

* * * *

August 30, 1887

Dear Lizzie,

I cannot believe that only two days ago I wrote you that miserable letter, and all has changed so completely! Where am I to begin? It started yesterday. I was sitting on the beach, sketching, and William came by, and stopped, and spoke to me. He told me the sketches were fine! Then he asked if I might like to go for a walk with him after supper, down to see the lobstermen come in. Oh, Lizzie, I could barely eat, I was so excited! I put on my blue and white dress, the one with the sailor collar, and I waited for him on the porch, because I was so afraid he would knock on the door and Mama would know! We walked through town down to the pier. At first I could barely speak, I kept thinking over and over that it must be a dream! But then I straightened out, and thought to myself that if I didn't speak, this dream would surely end and not come again, so I pulled myself together and began to listen to him, instead of thinking of myself. Before I knew it, we were having a true conversation! We spoke of everything, he told me all about his plans for his art and how he hopes to have a one-man show at Avery Galleries in New York next year. He asked me about my own dreams, Lizzie, and I managed not to appear too stupid, I think. We talked and talked for hours. The lobstermen came and went and we still sat on the pier talking! I got back home about 10:00 but it felt like midnight. At the very end, when we got back to our cottage, he touched my hand just for a moment, and said he could not remember a more delightful evening! Oh, Lizzie, I thought I would die with happiness!

And then today, he came by as soon as he got back from his day's work, and Mama was surprised, I can tell you that! He walked right into the kitchen and asked me to walk out with him again, which we did, and I just got back, and I had to write before another thing happened. Tonight we met up with Frank and Hugh Jones, and they talked with us, and included me as if it was the most natural thing in the world. Oh, Lizzie, do you think I am accepted as Will's girl now? (He asked me to call him Will, as he prefers it to William.) It all seems too much to believe! And yet I feel, deep in my heart, that I am his now, and always will be. Have I gone mad? It is just two evenings! Yet I feel so much from him, Lizzie, I cannot be imagining it.

How shall I tell Nellie and Minnie? They are bound to know by tomorrow. I think I must tell them before they hear it somehow. Is it a dream, Lizzie? Can anyone be this happy?

How I wish you were here! How I wish you could see it!

Love,

Gertrude

* * * *

September 12, 1887

Dear Lizzie,

You must think me very trying for not answering your letter right away, and my only defense is that so much keeps happening that I barely have time to think, much less write. Still, I apologize, for I know you are on pins and needles. I did go see Nellie and Minnie the very next day, when I was sure Will would have left to paint. I stood in their living room, and blushed and stammered, and tried to find a graceful way of saying it, when all of a sudden Nellie burst out laughing and they both ran to hug me. They already knew! Will had told them all, even his mother, the previous night. Then you can imagine my guilt at not confiding in Mama, so I had to tell her right away. And Lizzie, she did not faint away or get embarrassed, or do any of the things I had imagined would happen. No, she held my hands in her own, and said she was happy for me, and that he was a fine man. And I thought of Papa, Lizzie, and how brave Mama is without him, and how good, and loving. She loved him so much, and I could see in her eyes that she was remembering him, and wishing me as much happiness.

Everyone is happy for us, Lizzie, and now that people are beginning to know they treat me with kindness and respect. It is all so sudden, and yet it is all so definite. We seem to have leapt from acquaintances to courtship instantly. I am so comfortable with him, I respect him so completely. Surely he will marry me, won't he? Could any two people feel this much and not get married?

I don't know how I shall bear the winter without him. He promises to write everyday. I wish he did not have to go back to England, but his career makes it necessary. He has made many commitments to friends and colleagues, and he finds the season in London to be exhilarating. Lizzie, I am a bit intimidated about the circles he travels in when abroad. Queen Victoria has admired his paintings! Do you think I can learn to be a gracious and sophisticated hostess? I feel very young sometimes. But Will will surely teach me.

We will be home in ten days. For once, I do not look forward to it!

With all my love,

Gertrude

*   *   *   *

September 15, 1887

Dear Lizzie,

I know I will see you in a week, but I could not wait to tell you. Will has asked Mama and me to come to England for six weeks this winter, with Mrs. Picknell and Nellie. (Minnie and George can't come, they have too many other commitments.) Mama has accepted! Will wants to introduce us to his friends, and show us all of the sights. We are to go to the theatre, and all of the art shows, and anything else my heart desires, he promises. As soon as I get home we must begin getting my wardrobe together - you will have to help me with the latest European fashions. Oh, Lizzie, my happiness would be complete except for one thing - we must leave right after the opening of his exhibition at Williams and Everett's Gallery, right before Christmas. How we will miss you all! I cannot imagine Christmas without Ida and Frank. Do you think they will forgive me? At least we can make the wreaths together before I leave. But Christmas morning will not be the same without all of you... I could cry if I was not so happy!

Everything is a whirl, Lizzie. It will be so comforting to be home with you. You can put your arms around me and tell me that it is not a dream, and give me sensible advice and make all these changes seem easy to handle. You are my rock, Lizzie, I don't know what I would do without you.

Your loving little sister,

Gertrude

P.S. Do you think if George Francis had lived we would all be close? How I envy you knowing our brother, even though the memory is also painful. I wish he hadn't died in the War. I would love to have an older brother's advice now. Or Papa's.

Do you think Mama and Papa would have had me if George Francis had lived?

Eleanor stopped reading. She had already read more than enough letters to confirm her suspicions about Gertrude and William Lamb Picknell, but that was not what made her stop. It was something else. A strange coincidence.

Eleanor had been conceived in the grief following the death of an older sister - a fact she only found out when she was a teenager. No one ever spoke of her sister, Maryann's, death. She had drowned in a lake during a summer vacation. A freak accident. The family had been devastated. So much so, that they moved out of town and destroyed any evidence that she had ever existed. When Eleanor was born, they pretended she was the only girl. They thought they were protecting her, somehow. They didn't want her to think of herself as a substitute. She too, seemed to sense there was a secret she shouldn't know. There were many times along the way when someone almost said something, clues she could have picked up on if she'd cared too, but she'd also found herself participating in the deceit, yet not really knowing what it was she was hiding. When she'd found out the truth (her brother John took it upon himself to tell her one day - he claimed he could no longer stand the lies), she had been so hurt and confused that she had to go to counseling for months. She hated that time of her life. Hated it enough to swear never to go to counseling again, as if it was her therapist's fault that she was so miserable, not her own family's.

Eleanor did not dwell on that now. She thought of the strange fact that Gertrude, also, had been conceived in response to a sibling's death. That Gertrude, also, had loved an older, relatively famous man, named William. That the man died young... Goosebumps rose on her arm. Silly. It was just a coincidence.

She suddenly felt very tired. Too tired to read any more letters. She listened to the rain on the roof. *Go to Peter, go to Peter*, she imagined it tapping out. *Yes, I will, as soon as I take a little nap...* she promised the rain. Eleanor fell asleep, the letters tucked protectively under her arms.

* * * *

Eleanor woke a few hours later. The rain had stopped. She had a confused memory of a dream - a dream in which she was a little girl again and her sister Maryann played with her, but they were twins. They danced and ran and laughed in the backyard, and then Maryann disappeared, and her mother came out and scolded her, asking sternly, "What happened to Gertrude?" even though her sister's name was Maryann. But Eleanor woke up before she could answer.

For a few moments she was disoriented, wondering what time it was and why she was still dressed, instead of in her nightgown. Then she remembered that it was day, and she and Peter had quarreled. Wearily, she got up and went to Peter's door. She knocked gently.

There was no answer. "Peter?" she called tentatively. No reply. *Perhaps he's asleep*, she thought, and quietly opened the door.

Peter was gone. She turned to walk downstairs, calling "Peter!" as she went, but she already knew he wasn't going to be home. There was a note on the

kitchen counter: "Went out. Back by dinner. Peter."
How like him, she thought. *Here he is, furious with me,
but he doesn't want me to worry too much, so he leaves me
a note anyway.* Gertrude's words slowly floated back
through her mind. "You are my rock, Lizzie." Was
she Peter's rock? She shivered. It was a scary thought.

The phone rang. "Mom? Hey, it's me. I'm at
Nathan's. I'm sorry about before."

"No, Peter, I'm the one who should apologize.
I'm sorry I blew up at you. We... we can talk about it
later."

"Nathan wants to know if you want to come to
over here for dinner. He's got some lobsters."

Mmmm. Lobster. She hadn't tasted a fresh
lobster in two years. She loved them. "Sure. Tell him
I'll be right over."

Eleanor hung up the phone and realized she was
starving. *I have to shower. Maybe I'll put on a dress.* She
felt relieved, lighthearted. *Thank God Peter's not still
mad at me*, she thought, even though she knew that
nothing had changed, nothing was resolved.

＊　＊　＊　＊

"Feel better?" Nathan asked Peter.

"A little. Thanks for inviting her. She loves
lobster."

"I hope she knows how long they cook. I can
never remember. Okay, boys, close your eyes... I think
the water's just about boiling..." He tossed three
lobsters into the pot, slammed down the lid, counted to

52

ten, and took the lid off. "After all these years I still hate doing that!" he admitted. Peter laughed.

"You husk the corn, Peter. I'm going to make a salad. Does your Mom drink wine?"

Peter smiled. "Not often. But I'll bet she could use a drink after today."

"Don't worry too much about the fight, Peter. At least you broke the ice. Now maybe you two will talk more."

"I hope so. I hope I didn't just get her defenses up. She doesn't like to talk about difficult things."

"No one does. Give her time. But don't let her off the hook. She needs you to make her deal with things."

Peter thought about that while he peeled away the silk from some ears of white corn.

* * * *

Eleanor stepped out of the shower and stood, dripping, in front of her closet. *Hmmm. Where is that summer dress, the flowered one?* she asked herself. *Ahh, there.* She dried herself off and stepped back into the bathroom. She applied deodorant and body lotion, smoothing it over her legs, which she had just shaved for the first time in a week. She glanced in the mirror, paused, and then leaned her elbows upon the counter and really looked at herself. She had always been considered pretty. *I look old*, she thought. Her face looked tired, her green eyes had dark rings, she hadn't tweezed her eyebrows in months, there were a few grey hairs kinking out of her auburn hair. She yanked them out. *Better.* She tweezed. *Now some makeup.* She had to hunt through her makeup bag for powders that hadn't dried up from disuse. But when she was done, she was somewhat mollified by the results. She didn't look too awful.

A voice in the back of her mind was asking why she was going to so much trouble, but she was afraid to address it. If she thought about the fact that she was attempting to look nice for someone, another man, she would undoubtedly begin to cry. So she pretended it was the most natural thing in the world. Like the old days, when she always used to try to look her best.

She finished dressing and skipped down the stairs, feeling like a girl again. Jasmine meowed at her by the front door. "I'll bring you back a treat, Jasmine. Stay inside a while longer." Eleanor grabbed her keys and purse and left the house, thinking she would drive to Nathan's although it was only a few streets away. That way, she wouldn't get mud on her shoes or legs from walking.

But when she pulled up into Nathan's driveway, she was suddenly afraid to get out. She felt totally foolish, all dressed up. What would Peter think? It was too late to turn back, so reluctantly she got out of the car and knocked on Nathan's front door.

Nathan's house was cool white clapboard, in Cape Ann style, accented with an antique black trim. It was small and neat, and located in the heart of town, right on River Road. From upstairs one could see the point, and across the cove to Wingaersheek Beach. Nathan's backyard was as tidy as the house, with a white picket fence, manicured lawn and flower beds bordering three sides. A sculptured bird bath ornamented the center of the lawn. Nathan had purchased the house from his great-uncle when the older man had to go into a nursing home, and everyone in town was pleased that such a fine property had remained within the family.

It was Peter who answered the door. He smiled shyly when he noticed her appearance. From the kitchen Eleanor could hear Nathan struggling with the lobster pot. "You're just in time," he called out. "I think these lobsters are done."

Eleanor gave Peter an awkward hug, not quite sure how to apologize to him again. She squeezed his hand and walked by him into the kitchen. She felt safer in Nathan's presence. "You look nice!" he commented when she walked in.

"Thank you. It was very nice of you to invite me."

"We had a feeling you could use a lobster dinner." Nathan winked at Peter. Eleanor was grateful to see that Nathan knew about the fight, but obviously didn't hate her for it. She wasn't up to explanations, and she didn't want to spend the evening pretending she and Peter were completely at ease. Nathan's knowing gave her a sense of relief, somehow made it all seem like normal family disagreements. She noted that Peter, also, seemed very comfortable in Nathan's presence.

"If you don't mind grabbing the salad and bringing it into the dining room, I think we're ready to eat," Nathan announced. Peter carried a water pitcher, but Eleanor was charmed to see a bottle of Pinot Grigio and two wineglasses on the table for her and Nathan.

The dining room had a nautical theme, which

kept it from being very formal. The buffet table boasted a number of large scrimshaw items, a ship's steering wheel decorated the wall, and the lighting was provided by kerosene lanterns. Fishing spears also provided decorative accents. The table itself was a huge slab of polished driftwood, and the chairs were decorated with scrimshaw horns. It reminded Eleanor of a whaling boat galley, only more whimsical. She was intrigued. "Did your uncle do this?" she asked.

"No," Nathan replied. "It's from my antique whaling phase. One day I got it into my head that I wanted the dining room to look like one of those fake shipboard restaurants down on the wharf in Boston harbor. Decorators usually cringe when they see it, but I had a ball buying antiques and placing them around the room. I am kind-of proud of the table and chairs, though. A ladyfriend of mine made the table, and I salvaged the chairs from a buddy's attic. His wife had decided to redo their house in ultra-contemporary. Chrome and leather. She thought the chairs were eyesores, but I agree and love them anyway."

Eleanor smiled across the table. She'd always thought Nathan was very nice, but it was surprising to find out how interesting he was. Very self-confident and self-deprecating at the same time. It was a refreshing quality. She liked people who could laugh at themselves but marched to their own drummer anyway. Bill was like that.

"I think this room is great," Peter piped in. "Captain Ahab would be at home here."

"Have you actually read Moby Dick?" Nathan asked him.

"Had to. Eighth grade reading assignment."

"Really?" Eleanor asked, surprised. "I didn't

know you read that last year. Pretty difficult reading for eighth grade, I think."

"Some of the kids had trouble with it, but I liked it." Eleanor looked at Peter, impressed. Her son was a source of constant amazement. "Your Dad would be impressed. It was one of his favorite books, too."

Peter looked pleased, and Eleanor felt that perhaps she'd made up, a little bit, for the way she'd spoken earlier in the day.

"I might be a writer when I grow up, too," he stated. Here was another surprise. Eleanor had no idea he was interested in writing.

Nathan was pouring the wine. "It always helps to read the classics if you want to be a great writer. It's the same with artists. They always study the old masters before they find their own path. You can learn a lot from the triumphs of those before you," he said.

"I never read my Dad's books until after he died. I always thought they'd be over my head. I guess they are a little bit, but I think I understand enough of them to wish I could ask him about them. I would never have waited if I'd known he was going to die so young."

There was a moment of silence, then Eleanor sighed. "I'm ashamed to admit I didn't know you read your Dad's books either. You could ask me about them, sometime. I met your Dad at a writing seminar, and he talked a lot about his work in the course. And I should be able to answer your questions about the more recent books. He used to love to talk about the plots while he was writing. He'd get excited about an idea and describe it in detail to me before he'd even written a word. I was always fascinated with the way he came up with his ideas and then worked them all out in his head. He made it all seem like fun, but I know the stories had very deep meanings to him. Unfortunately, it was easier for him to talk about the stories, than what they meant to him. He was such a creative writer that you can get lost in the art of his work, without ever getting to the purpose behind it."

"Mom, I only understand about half of what you just said," Peter laughed. "But I will ask you about them sometime. I didn't know you met Dad in a writing class."

While Eleanor recounted the story of their meeting, Nathan looked on at the two of them, very pleased. They were obviously beginning to make some progress. He suddenly had an idea. "Why don't the three of us take my boat out this weekend?" he asked when there was a break in the conversation.

"Can we Mom?" Peter asked excitedly.

"Sure, sounds like fun," Eleanor answered. "I'll pack us some lunch," she added, a bit shyly. Throughout the rest of the conversation she was quieter, wondering what she was doing. Was she spending too much time with Nathan? Was he just being friendly, or would he think she was interested in him in a romantic way? *Was* she interested in him in a romantic way? She felt a hollow feeling in the pit of her stomach, although she continued to eat the lobster with relative pleasure. She was disrupted from her reverie by the sudden realization that she'd been asked a question, and two expectant faces were waiting for her reply.

"What? I'm sorry, I was sidetracked for a moment."

"We were just asking if you wanted to take the

boat up to Newburyport."

"Oh, I'd love to. I've never been there."

"Really?" Nathan asked. "You'll like it. It's charming. We'll do lunch up there; they've got some great restaurants."

It was settled then. They'd spend the day together on the boat on Sunday, assuming the weather was fine (Peter and Nathan reserved Saturday to catch up with the work they'd missed today). After dinner, the three of them took care of the dishes with haste, and then Eleanor insisted that she and Peter had to be going.

In the car on the way home, Peter said, "I had fun tonight." Eleanor, strangely, thought that the statement was almost a challenge, one she had to answer.

"I did too," she admitted. But she wondered why it was so important to Peter that she'd had a good time. Was this what he had meant earlier about her getting out and enjoying life, or was he secretly hoping that something would blossom between her and Nathan? She hoped it was only the former, and not the latter, because it hurt her to think that Peter could think so lightly of her love, that it could be transferred to another man so easily. It never occurred to her that perhaps Peter didn't think you had to stop loving one person, in order to love another.

4

Eleanor woke up the next morning in the mood to clean. It was a very small thing, but deep down inside her she knew it was a sign - a tiny sign that she was interested in life. It had been ages and ages since she'd woken up wanting to do anything. Usually she woke up disappointed that she hadn't passed away from a broken heart during the night.

She was greeted downstairs by an anxious Jasmine, who had been treated to lobster roe the evening before and had been promised more in the morning. Eleanor scooped a healthy spoonful into a bowl, and plopped it down on the kitchen floor. Jasmine ate the delicacy slowly, savoring every nibble.

Eleanor hugged herself with excitement. It was Thursday, which meant the Historical Society would be open in the evening. *Perhaps I'll find out tonight who Gertrude and Lizzie are.* She hoped it wasn't a difficult process. She still felt fragile about anything difficult.

Peter skipped off to work with Nathan, and Eleanor spent the day dusting, vacuuming, and scrubbing down every room in the cottage. There actually wasn't too much work - a cleaning service had been visiting the house every two weeks the entire time it was unoccupied - but when she had finished there was a great sense of satisfaction nevertheless. She remembered her mother telling her when she was a child: "No one will ever take care of your property as well as you will." It was true; so what if it was also a convenient excuse for not hiring help when you really couldn't afford it anyway.

Eleanor's family had always been less "comfortable" than their neighbors', a fact which Eleanor had come to realize had less to do with their industriousness than with the sense of guilt and shame with which the death of their first daughter had burdened them. This kept them, afterwards, from ever really feeling that they deserved good fortune, which in turn kept them from ever actually pursuing it. There had been opportunities, Eleanor recalled, when her father could have applied to move up in the company, but she remembered him telling her mother, knowingly, that there were others who would surely be preferred by the bosses. Her mother never argued, just turned her face away guiltily and responded, "Yes, yes, I'm sure your right."

Eleanor, however, saw from the example of her older brothers that those who went after things often got them, for both of her siblings managed to move up the corporate ladder fairly quickly, partly based on their willingness to relocate wherever the better jobs were. Of course they wanted to escape from home, and the quiet sense of defeat that always hung over the household. Luckily, they did not forget to pull Eleanor along with them; it was her brothers who mainly financed her education, and enabled her to attend the summer seminar at Harvard. Once she had married "well," they pretty much considered their responsibility towards her through. The goal had never been any particular success for her, only that she be able, like them, to get away from home.

Eleanor told herself not to think so much. Thoughts of her childhood always made her sad - a different kind of sad than thoughts of Bill - a sad that was soft, permanent, useless. What was the use of feeling sorry for her parents? They were victims of themselves more than of any external event. There was an irony in her thinking this, but she was unable to see it.

Eleanor decided to skip reading a new letter, but instead to review the ones she'd already read, so they would be fresh in her mind when she got to the Historical Society. She made a mental list of questions:

1. Who are Gertrude and Lizzie Johnson, and how are they related to Bill's family?

2. Were there once houses on the point?

3. What did Gertrude mean by "the twin?"

4. What information did they have on William Lamb Picknell?

Eleanor arrived at the door of the Historical Society promptly at seven p.m. It was a small white clapboard building on Leonard Street, the main street in Annisquam, and one of only a few buildings that had any public function at all, yet Eleanor had never been inside it before. She had meant to stop in, many times, but her summer days in Annisquam had always been lazy, filled with beach picnics, sailing excursions, and dinners in Rockport or barbecues with friends. And the Historical Society was open such irregular hours, that whenever she thought about visiting it was invariably closed.

As she pushed open the door she remembered that Lydia had warned her to telephone first, and as she walked in she could immediately see why. The main room was filled with photo albums, scrapbooks, filing cabinets, and closets bulging with information. There was a completely haphazard look about all of it, as if people were constantly adding to the collection but no one had the time to organize it. Sitting amidst a pile of old papers and photographs was a young woman - *probably no older than twenty-five or twenty-six*, Eleanor thought - with a puzzled expression on her face. She had short blond hair, blue eyes, and a determined chin. She turned and flashed a dazzling smile at Eleanor.

"Thank goodness you're here!" she stated, as if they were old friends. "I can't make heads or tails of any of this and I'm desperate for an excuse to stop trying!"

Eleanor was slightly taken aback, but charmed nevertheless. The young woman exuded enthusiasm.

"I'm Eleanor Strayer. I found some old letters and I'm trying to find out some information about them."

"Oh, I know your family! Bill Strayer, the writer, right? We were all so sad when he died. I'm Gabrielle Newsome, Gabby, Tom Newsome's daughter. My Dad's not here tonight, so you'll have to make do with me. He knows everything about Annisquam, but I like to think I'm a fast learner. So tell me about these letters?"

With quick dispatch, Eleanor related all the pertinent details. Her earlier reticence about the letters completely disappeared, and she told this energetic stranger everything she could remember that might help answer her questions. Gabby nodded periodically, and was surprisingly full of information.

"There were houses on the point. A bunch of

cottages, and some of them were twins - you know, two cottages exactly the same. Those that survived were eventually moved up into the hills during the twentieth century, because the owners got tired of repairing storm damage. When the ferry stopped running from the point across to Coffin's beach (we call it Wingaersheek now), living on the point wasn't an advantage anymore."

"Can you tell if our cottage was moved up from the point?"

"Not without going into Salem to do a title search. Unless you can recognize it from some old photographs."

Gabby pulled a box towards her and started sifting through its contents. "I think there are a couple of good pictures in here somewhere... Ah, here's a few!"

Eleanor looked them over. At first she didn't see anything familiar, and then suddenly she exclaimed, "Yes, that's our house! I recognize the front door. See how it comes right up to the first windows? Mary always said our cottage was unique that way, except for the one next door... Next door! Of course, the twin."

Gabby was pleased she had been able to help. "Who's Mary?" she asked.

"Bill's mother. We inherited the cottage from them. But they've never heard of a Lizzie Johnson. Have you?"

"No...," Gabby answered slowly, considering. "Let's look in the town directories."

There was no William Johnson listed in the 1880s. "They could have been summer renters, you know, in which case they won't be listed" Gabby advised Eleanor. "You really need Gertrude's last name to be sure, though. Perhaps it was her family that owned the cottage, since Johnson is a married name."

"That's a good point."

"It's definitely worth a trip to Salem. You can find out everything about your cottage there."

"What about the artist, William Lamb Picknell? Do you have any information about him here?"

"Let's see, where to look? Try that filing cabinet to your right - - look under "Artists" as well as his name. I'll take a look at these photograph albums over here, I think some artists are in them."

There was a small manila file for "William Lamb Picknell." Inside were some press clippings, mainly about artists working in Annisquam, in which he often was listed most prominently. But then a small blurb caught her eye:

April 19, 1889

Two of our summer residents were married yesterday in Waltham, Massachusetts. William Lamb Picknell, whose paintings of our shores have won honors both here and abroad, married Miss Gertrude Powers, a longtime summer visitor and cousin to the Langdon family, which includes Miss Katherine Langdon, also a local artist. The ceremony took place at the First Parish Church of Waltham. We look forward to giving them personal felicitations when they arrive for the summer season.

Now she knew Gertrude's last name: *Powers*. Before she had time to bring it to Gabby's attention, Gabby herself was calling out with excitement: "Oh, look at this! It's a picture with all of them in it!"

Gabby was holding a large, browned photograph of a group of people sitting on a cottage porch - Eleanor's cottage. To her delight, a number of names had been penciled in on the back, each corresponding with a sitter on the front. In the bottom row sat two children, a boy and a girl, who had been identified as "Frank" and "Me." The three people seated together in the middle of the second row were identified as George Picknell, Minnie Picknell and William Picknell; while on the top row were identifications for Nellie Picknell, "Aunt Gertrude," and "Mama." Eleanor was bursting with excitement. "Look, that's Gertrude and 'Mama' is Lizzie and the little girl has to be Ida! I can't believe you came up with this photograph, this is amazing!"

Eleanor was mesmerized by Gertrude. She was looking off to the side instead of the camera, as if her glance was arrested by something in the distance at the last moment. She had an interesting face - large, wide-set eyes that gave her almost an exotic look. Like all the women, her hair was tucked neatly in a bun, but unlike the others her dress had no flowers, or stripes, or ornamentation. She was wearing a simple dark skirt and white blouse, with a scarf around her neck that looked more like a man's tie than a graceful bow. She was sitting next to Nellie, and holding the hand of the woman to her left (*perhaps cousin Katherine?* Eleanor thought) but her posture was stiff, not relaxed, as if she planned to jump up and run off as soon as she could. "She looks every bit the tomboy she apparently was," Eleanor told Gabby.

"When do you suppose it was taken?" Gabby asked.

"Well, she and William don't seem particularly familiar, so it must be from before they were a couple. Hey, maybe it was taken in 1886! I remember that Gertrude asked her brother-in-law to bring a camera that summer, to take a picture of all of the summer residents together. Yes, that makes sense, the picture must have been taken by Lizzie's family, or Ida wouldn't have owned it."

"Wow. You really know a lot about them. Who do you suppose these other people are?"

"I don't know. That one might be Katherine Langdon," Eleanor speculated, pointing to the woman beside Gertrude, "She was their cousin and an artist, although you'd think Ida would have identified her. Those two who look like brothers might be the Jones brothers, I suppose," she added, pointing to two well-dressed young men sitting near to William.

Gabby looked hard at William. "He's not exactly your romantic type, is he?" she noted to Eleanor.

William Lamb Picknell was dressed in a light brown suit and a straw hat. He had a broad face, big ears, and a large, sweeping black moustache. Yet he looked intelligent, and kind. "But I like him," Eleanor announced. Yes, he and Gertrude must have made a very interesting couple.

"Can I get a xerox of this photograph?" Eleanor asked.

"I can do better than that. I'll let you make a copy if you swear not to tell my Dad. You look trustworthy."

Eleanor smiled. She liked Gabby. She couldn't remember the last time she'd met someone she liked as much. "Oh, I almost forgot," Eleanor told her. "I found this newspaper article about Gertrude and William Picknell's marriage, and it contains her last name: Powers."

Gabby grabbed the town directories again. "Nope. No Powers."

"Try Langdon. That's their cousins' name."

"Voila!" Gabby declared. "Here they are. They owned a house on Cambridge Road. Cambridge Road goes down to the Point, so they probably owned the cottages too, and rented them out."

"I wonder if Bill's family is descended from the Langdons, or if they purchased the cottage from them at some point?"

"Well, listen, I have to go to Salem next week," Gabby announced. "Why don't I try to figure out the history of the cottage for you?"

"Really? I hate for you to do all that work for me."

"Then come with me! We'll make a day of it. Have lunch and all. Actually, I'd love the company. It's pretty boring work plowing through all those old records. Having someone to talk to would make the day go faster."

They agreed on a tentative date of Tuesday, and Eleanor gave Gabby her phone number. "Thanks for your help," she added, clutching the photograph.

"No problem! See you next week!"

Eleanor rushed home, eager to look at the photograph again and contemplate everything she'd discovered.

* * * *

The next morning Eleanor was up with the sun and determined to find a photographer who could copy her old photograph. A quick browse through the yellow pages confirmed her suspicion that for the right service she'd have to drive almost all the way back to Boston. She decided that as long as she was going to be near a mall anyway, it wouldn't hurt to pick up a few new cosmetics and some hair color.

But after she'd copied the photograph, Eleanor began to get cold feet. What in the world did she need cosmetics and hair color for? Sunday's sail with Nathan loomed on the horizon and filled her with confusion. Surely she was not going to this trouble for *him*? What would be the point? She had sworn to herself, to Bill in his grave, many, many times, that she would never love another man again, that she would hold a torch for him for the rest of her life, and die happy knowing she was going to soon be with him. And then they'd be reunited in heaven... This was how she coped with the reality of his death and her now meaningless life. If she began to abandon this view of the world, did it mean she never really loved Bill enough in the first place?

Eleanor pulled into the parking lot of the mall and sat in the car, her heart beating fast and her forehead breaking out into a cold sweat. *Am I having a panic attack?* she wondered. After a few moments she managed to calm herself down. *It's only cosmetics*, she reminded herself. *It wouldn't hurt you to look nice for your son.* This was the argument that got her into Macy's, and up to the cosmetics counter.

She was so confused and torn about what she wanted that she was simply ignored by the saleswoman for Lancôme, who couldn't be bothered with anyone not savvy enough to know what they were looking for. The saleswoman for Estée Lauder, however, saw Eleanor as a golden opportunity, and called her over. "Madam, may I help you over here? Perhaps you'd like to try out a few items. We have some new colors for the summer season."

Grateful to be led around, Eleanor walked over and proceeded to let the woman brush colors, one after another, onto her hand, until she'd developed a color scheme that she declared would bring out the highlights in Eleanor's hair and skin:

"Some cool browns, I think, for your green eyes, with just a touch of pink. And plum blush, a little rosy. A pink lipstick, but not hot. Cool, with a liner just a shade darker. There, lets try it on your face."

Eleanor had to admit the effect was pretty. It had been a long time since she'd felt pretty. Was it a terrible thing, to look pretty instead of depressed and mournful? Maybe... she didn't want anyone to think she was happy. She was not happy. She was a young widow. But Peter would be so pleased if she looked better...

"Thank you. I'll take it. And a mascara."

"Go for the darkest brown," the saleswoman suggested. "Black can look jarring."

"And my hair..." Eleanor began.

"We have a salon in the store, if you're interested. I can call over and get you an appointment right away."

"No, thank you," Eleanor answered, this time with conviction, because she knew if she started with salon color, she'd be committed for good. "But if you can point me in the direction of a pharmacy, where they sell hair color products..."

The saleswoman leaned over the counter and spoke conspiratorially. "There's a drug store in the mall. Try L'Oreal's medium auburn shade. It covers well and would be perfect on you. A friend of mine uses it and swears it conditions better than the other brands."

"Thank you, I'll try what you suggest." Eleanor really was grateful. The saleswoman had probably just spared her hours of looking at boxes of hair color in confusion.

When she arrived back at the cottage with her purchases, it was still early afternoon. The weather was beautiful, and Eleanor was reluctant to spend the day indoors, even though she was eager to try coloring her hair. *I promised Grace I'd report on my visit to the Historical Society*, she remembered. *I'll just grab a bite to eat and walk down to her house.*

Grace Pippin lived on Leonard Street near the fork for Walnut, in a large Victorian house that had been in her family since the 19th century. Grace was the last of the Pippins still living in Annisquam, and Eleanor often wondered if she was lonely now in that home that had in her childhood harbored two parents, eight children, occasional cousins, numerous pets, plus servants and frequent visitors. But for Grace, living with her memories within walls that had borne them witness was far preferable to living anywhere else. She was the only child who had married locally, and the only one who never had any children, which in Yankee logic had qualified her to inherit the house from her parents, who trusted her to keep it an open haven for all of her siblings and numerous nieces and nephews. Her family had been good to her; she was unconcerned with upkeep or repairs, for these same nieces and nephews (and grandnieces and grandnephews now) were appropriately grateful for summer vacation in this huge old Annisquam landmark, and generously made sure the house stayed in good shape.

Eleanor rang the doorbell and was ushered in by Miss Wilkins, a rather withered-looking old woman who came twice a week to tidy up. Their situation was somewhat amusing, as Miss Wilkins was almost as old as Grace herself, and certainly by all appearances didn't have half of Grace's energy. Nevertheless, Grace had been using her services for so long that she now declared herself "used to her," which at her age meant it would take an act of God to get her to make any change in the arrangement.

Grace was sitting in the sun room, a back porch that looked out over the extensive garden, and truly was the only room in the house that could appropriately be described as sunny. The rest of the house, in typical Victorian fashion, was filled with furniture, knickknacks and paintings, and bore heavy curtains and flower-patterned wallpapered walls. Eleanor always felt as if she was walking into the past when she entered the house.

Grace was delighted to see her and said so. Eleanor accepted her offer of a pretty, chintz-covered chair, and Miss Wilkins went to make tea and see what she could find in the cupboard.

"I've been to the Historical Society," Eleanor began, "and it was well worth the trip."

"Tell me about your letters. What were you looking for?"

Eleanor told Grace what she knew about Gertrude, and about Gertrude's courtship with

William Lamb Picknell. When she mentioned the Langdon family, Grace perked up.

"I remember them!" Grace exclaimed. "Oh, they were a nice family. Always had company visiting them, so that it was hard to tell who was actually a part of their family and who was just a perennial guest."

"Did you know that they owned two cottages on the point?" Eleanor inquired.

"No. That must have been before my time."

"Well, our cottage was once on the point, and the Langdons apparently owned it. At some time the cottage was moved to its present location. I'm going to Salem next week with Gabby Newsome to figure out if Bill's family is descended from the Langdons, or if they sold the cottage to them."

"Gabby is a nice girl. The Historical Society is her father's baby. If it wasn't for him I think it might have closed years ago, and been incorporated into the Library. But he's been tenderly nurturing it for years, trying to make some sense out of all the materials there."

"Well, it's a treasure-trove of ephemera. Gabby found an old photograph of Gertrude, her sister's family, and the Picknell family all sitting on the steps of our cottage - I couldn't believe it existed. Then I found a newspaper clipping about their marriage."

"How nice for Gertrude to have married her first love," Grace remarked. "It's so rare these days."

"I did," Eleanor noted.

"Really? Well, that was quite unusual wasn't it? Goodness knows I had a few loves before I married Walter, and a few more afterwards too," Grace added with a twinkle in her eye.

Eleanor was truly shocked. Grace and Walter

were famous for their devotion to each other, and Grace had never remarried. "You fell in love with other men after Walter passed away?" she asked incredulously.

"Goodness, you make it sound scandalous!" Grace protested. "Of course I did. I was only sixty years old when Walter died. Ellie, you don't expect to spend the rest of your life in mourning, do you?"

"No..., I don't," Eleanor said, without much conviction. *I will if I want to*, she thought to herself.

Grace leaned over and took her hand. "Ellie, I was devastated when Walter died. He was my partner, my best friend. I missed him very much. But eventually, I let other people into my life. Walter would have wanted me to be happy, Ellie. He wouldn't have wanted me to mope for the past twenty years!"

Shyly, Eleanor asked, "How long did it take, until, you know, you started having feelings for someone else?"

Grace hesitated a moment before answering. "Not too long I suppose. The human heart is like the sea, Ellie. If it finds a hole it wants to fill it up."

The conversation was interrupted by the arrival of Miss Wilkins with tea and cookies. The interruption allowed Grace to bring up what she suspected was a sensitive subject.

"You know, you have Peter to think about. That must be a comfort. I very much regretted not having children, when Walter was no longer with me."

Eleanor sighed. "Peter and I don't get along very well. I think he's mad at me."

"Goodness, why Ellie?"

"I don't know. He wants me to be happy, and

I'm not."

"A perfectly logically request on his part," Grace observed. "He loves you, so of course it hurts him to see you sad."

"Yes, but he thinks I should just get on with my life. How do I do that? I don't know what that means. My life was with Bill, now it isn't. What do I replace that with?"

Grace looked at Eleanor very seriously, and Eleanor instinctively squirmed. "Ellie, think about what you just said. Why, your happiness was never dependent on Bill, it was always only dependent on you. You have to choose to be happy. You have to choose your next path. Nothing and no one can replace Bill, but many other people and things can make you happy, if you let them."

Eleanor felt ashamed. Grace was echoing Peter's words. Eleanor was suddenly uncomfortably aware of her unwillingness to feel better, to move on. Tears filled her eyes. "You're right," she whispered.

Grace patted her hand. "Ellie, you're afraid. It's nothing to be ashamed of. We're all afraid. Don't let your fears paralyze you. Take small steps. It will get better, I promise."

"I'm sorry, Grace." Eleanor was now openly crying. "I'm so confused about everything. I used to know just what I was doing, at least I thought I did, but now I don't know what to do about anything. Everything overwhelms me, even small things, and it makes life so difficult. I want to be happy, I really do, but I don't know how."

"It's like I said, Ellie. Small steps. Take your time. But try everyday. I know one thing, Ellie, if I know anything. Bill wouldn't want you to be this way."

"You're right, I know." Eleanor dried her eyes. "Thank you."

"Dear, what you are going through is perfectly normal. It's just taking you a little longer to go through it."

Why? Eleanor asked herself. *Why is it so hard for me?* But she allowed Grace to change the subject, and they talked about gardens, and Lydia's most recent escapade, and when Miranda's children would be visiting. When Eleanor finally left, she felt infinitely better, and on the long walk home, she allowed herself to think that perhaps it was true - Bill wanted her to be happy.

* * * *

By the time Eleanor returned home, she had just enough time to color her hair before making dinner. The instructions said to leave the color mixture on the hair for thirty minutes. Thirty minutes was an ideal amount of time to devote to another letter.

Eleanor was not surprised to discover that the next letter was written from England. It was dated December 20, 1887, on fancy stationary from *The Adelphi Hotel* in Liverpool.

Dear Lizzie,

We have finally arrived! You can give William the satisfaction of knowing that he was right - the crossing was rough and miserable and we all got seasick!

Yes, even me, despite my brave boasts beforehand. I have never seen such waves in my life! You would think that a seasoned sailor like myself would be able to stand a little gale storm, wouldn't you? The only consolation to my pride is the fact that everyone was sick, right down to the Captain, who declared he'd rarely experienced a rougher sea. Poor Mama was afraid we'd all be drowned, but we were never really in any danger. Anyway, we are all recovering nicely in this beautiful hotel. Lizzie, I've never seen such an elegant place! The public spaces are all marble, with luxurious carpets, chandeliers and palms, and painted ceilings. On top of that, it is entirely decorated for the Christmas season, with wreaths and glitter everywhere. There are Turkish baths, swimming pools, squash courts, tennis courts and even a shooting gallery! We have our own bathroom, and the largest bed I've ever seen, which Mama and I are sharing. It is certainly an excellent way to recover from a long and miserable sea voyage.

We are to spend two days here and then go to Ealing to spend Christmas with the Wilkinsons. Will is absolutely bursting with the anticipation of introducing me to them, they are like a second family to him, and Hugh is like a brother. Will has been so sweet to me! Although in all honesty I must recount that we barely saw each other on the ship, since we were all mainly confined to our rooms. We were each too embarrassed to show our green faces to the other! But he has made up for it handsomely (he has apologized over and over again, by the way, as if the condition of the sea were his own fault!) and has been escorting me all over town, and showing me the sights. Tomorrow we are going to the Liverpool Gallery to see his painting! I am very proud to be on the arm of the artist who impressed Queen Victoria!

Ah, Lizzie, I do believe I am still a bit lightheaded and tired. I will write more from Ealing.

All my love,

Gertrude

P.S. In reading this over I realize I have barely mentioned Mama. She is fine, and in fact feels better than I do. She is becoming very chummy with Mrs. Picknell and the two of them have been shopping incessantly since we arrived on land. Needless to say all the presents are for you and the children! Tell Frank and Ida that I miss them very much, and love them with all my heart.

As Eleanor rinsed the color out of her hair, she wondered what the arrangements for Gertrude's trip had been. Who had paid the expenses? Were the two of them officially affianced at this point, and, if so, did that affect who paid? Idly she tried to imagine what would have been considered proper, but having very little information to go on, she was left curious. *I suppose there are some things I'll never know,* she realized. *I could do research from now until doomsday and there would still be things I could never discover.* She frowned at the thought, and wished there was some way to know Gertrude's story better. Then she laughed at herself. *It's another person, another lifetime,* she thought. *Why do I care so much about her?*

As Eleanor dried her hair, she forgot all about Gertrude. She just stared at herself. *I look pretty!* she thought, admiringly. She felt wonderful. She was honestly amazed at how good she looked. *You'd never know I went through a tragedy*, she thought.

Suddenly, to her horror, a vision passed before her eyes. She remembered Bill's face as she'd found him after the aneurysm. He'd looked cold and lifeless, his skin was bluish like a fish, and Eleanor had known even before she'd touched him that he was dead. It was as if someone had thrown cold water on her. *No*, she thought, *don't think about it*. But she was afraid to look in the mirror anymore.

She mechanically walked downstairs and made dinner, but even Peter's compliments on her hair couldn't shake the feeling of horror that haunted her. *I should have left well enough alone*, she thought. *What was the point of trying to look nice when the only person who matters can't see me anymore?*

For the rest of the evening, Eleanor was somber and absorbed in her own thoughts, and Peter was left to wonder what had set her off, and wish she was not unhappy again.

5

Saturday seemed endless to Eleanor. She spent the day on the beach reading an old copy of Louisa May Alcott's <u>Little Women</u>. Of course she had known the story by heart since childhood, but it was lighthearted, effortless reading - the kind she needed to keep her mind off of the impending boat excursion. Still, Eleanor felt fidgety, and her mind kept wandering away from the book and back to herself, and the uncomfortable feeling of nervousness with which she regarded the upcoming day. Her mind was in such a state of anxiety and anticipation that she actually forgot about Gertrude and her letters.

Sunday dawned beautiful, and promised to be eighty degrees with a nice breeze. Nathan had instructed them to meet him at the marina at ten o'clock. She knew he had to arrive early to make sure the boat was shipshape, and that everything they would need was on board. So she was not surprised to see him, suntan-lotioned and grinning, climbing up from below deck just as she and Peter approached down the wooden pier.

"Hey, can you believe this day? It's perfect!" he called out happily.

They climbed aboard, and Nathan told Eleanor

to find a comfortable spot and relax, while he showed Peter how to help with the masts. Peter proved more knowledgeable than Nathan expected, since Bill had taken him out sailing every summer since he'd been five. It was a thrill Peter had sorely missed, and he was delighted to be sailing once again with Nathan. Eleanor, too, loved to sail, but she hadn't exactly missed it. Rather, she had many times been grateful that Bill had sold the sailboat at the end of the summer just before he died, because he was anticipating buying a new one the next year. That coincidence had meant one less thing for Eleanor to take care of.

As they got underway it proved to be a wonderful day for sailing. The sky was blue, the sea was calm, but the breeze was brisk and steady. As the boat slowly rose and dipped over the water, Eleanor's anxiety was siphoned away with each wave they covered. She felt herself relax, yet she felt alive and exhilarated, as if her body, stretched out on the deck and rising and falling in tandem with the boat, was at one with the sea and the sky. It was a delicious feeling, one she didn't want to end. When they arrived in Newburyport so swiftly, after only an hour's sail, it was a disappointment.

Meanwhile Nathan and Peter had been chatting and managing the boat, Nathan letting Peter steer. They seemed to sense that Eleanor was happy, and didn't bother her at all, until it was necessary to rouse her from her reverie in order to get the boat into Newburyport harbor.

"Watch out for the boom, Eleanor, we're coming about. Okay, Peter, let down the sail. We'll motor in."

Eleanor stretched as she moved to the side of

the boat and looked with curiosity towards the harbor. The marina was surprisingly new and sophisticated for a town that had been founded in the seventeenth century. Nathan explained that a few decades back the whole waterfront had been re-done. "They almost razed the town at one point, it was such an eyesore. But instead, better heads prevailed and they restored it. It's one of my favorite places. Wait till you see the houses inland."

Nathan's plan for the day was to take a long walk about the residential streets before settling on a place for lunch, and then to spend part of the afternoon window shopping in the many galleries and boutiques that lined the downtown streets. Eleanor and Peter soon found that a tour about town with an architectural historian was infinitely more interesting than a tour without one. He pointed out houses from each historical period, and noted interesting architectural details and unusual touches. They walked for what seemed like miles, fascinated by everything Nathan had to say. By the time they got to the Coffin House, dating from 1654, they were on the edge of town and far from the harbor.

"I don't know about you, but I'm exhausted," Nathan suddenly declared.

"I'm starving," Peter piped in, and Eleanor agreed with both of them.

"We need a cab," Nathan said, but the possibility of seeing one seemed remote. Newburyport was far more of a residential, than a tourist, town.

Nathan, however, was of a practical mind, and far too used to being well-liked to consider the possible impropriety of what he did next. He simply stopped the next empty pickup truck that came along, and asked the driver to let them hop in until they got close to downtown, which the driver very graciously did. As they bumped down the road in the back of the truck, Eleanor reflected on Nathan's amazing self-confidence, and wondered what it must be like to go through life so sure that people will be happy to oblige you.

They shook hands heartily with the driver after arriving at their destination, and of course offered to pay him, which he of course refused. Either side would have been surprised if the other had not acted in exactly that way. Yankee hospitality and graciousness is a time-honored tradition on the North Shore.

With lunch the only problem left to solve, Nathan let Peter pick the restaurant. He chose Ciro's, in the Firehouse, because they could sit out on the back patio and overlook the harbor. Peter, like his father, never tired of the sea.

Eleanor ordered a salad with grilled shrimp, but the men ordered heartily: bruschetta, salads, lasagna, and tiramisu for dessert, which they insisted Eleanor share. About halfway through the meal Nathan asked casually what Eleanor had been up to the past week.

"I've been doing research on some old letters I found."

Both Nathan and Peter were quite surprised by this news. "What letters?" Peter demanded at the same time that Nathan inquired, "What kind of research?"

"Well, I found some letters in our attic from a Gertrude Powers to her sister Lizzie Johnson in the 1880s. I've been trying to figure out who they were and what they have to do with our cottage. Gertrude married an artist, William Lamb Picknell. It's very interesting."

"Have you been to the Historical Society?" Nathan asked.

"Uh-huh, I have. Gabby Newsome found some information for me, and we're going to Salem on Tuesday to do a title search on the cottage."

Peter looked thoughtful. "Is that Lizzie person the one you asked Grandma about?" he wanted to know.

Eleanor replied in the affirmative.

"Then why didn't you tell her why you wanted to know?"

"I don't know," Eleanor answered honestly. "At the time I had just found them, and for some reason I wanted to keep it a secret for a while. I know it's silly, but it was my first instinct."

"But now you've discovered that you need help to unravel the story," Nathan observed.

"Yes, but even so, I have a strange sort-of sense of privacy about the whole thing. I haven't even read them all; I only allow myself to read one letter a day. But that's because I know the end is sad and I'm not in a hurry to get to it."

"What happens in the end?" Peter asked, filled with curiosity.

"The artist, William Lamb Picknell, dies."

Peter and Nathan took in this information and exchanged a glance. They both felt a sense of alarm about Eleanor reading anything about someone dying, but Nathan, older and experienced, suspected that if Eleanor wanted to pursue the whole thing then it probably was a healthy instinct. Peter wasn't that sure.

"Can I read the letters?" he asked.

"I'm not done yet," Eleanor answered, although that was irrelevant.

"Then when you're done?" Peter pursued.

"No. You can't."

The finality with which she said this took even Eleanor by surprise. She felt protective - of what, she knew not, but a strong desire to keep the letters away from others' eyes had a hold of her, and she felt that with every grain of her being she would stick to her guns on this point. Peter was naturally offended. "Why not?" he demanded, and Eleanor gave Nathan a pleading look to help her get out of this.

"The letters are very old. Your Mom probably just worries about them tearing or something," he offered helpfully, although he too was puzzled by Eleanor's refusal to share them.

"She knows I'll be careful!" Peter protested.

"I know you would be," Eleanor said, "but the answer is still no."

For the rest of the meal Peter pouted. Eleanor knew she was being irrational and stubborn, but she couldn't change her mind. She couldn't share the letters with anyone.

Luckily, Peter eventually brightened as they traversed the shops and downtown streets after lunch. After a while he seemed to forget about being angry at his mother, for he filed it in his mind under those things which his mother did since the death that were incomprehensible. But Nathan was filled with curiosity about Eleanor's motives.

Sailing back home, he took the opportunity to climb up next to Eleanor, letting Peter man the boat alone. She was sitting upright, not relaxed as she'd been on the trip down, and was lost in thought, wondering at her passion for the letters, and chiding herself for ruining the day somewhat. So she was not the least surprised when Nathan asked her quietly, "Why *don't* you want Peter to read the letters?"

"I don't know Nathan, I honestly don't. They're just very personal to me. I can't explain it."

The boat sailed along a ways, and Nathan and Eleanor sat quietly. Finally, Eleanor seemed to remember herself and her surroundings. "Thank you for today. It was really splendid," she said, smiling.

"I had a good time too. Listen Eleanor, would you like to go out to dinner sometime? Just the two of us?"

Eleanor was taken completely by surprise by this, lost as she had been since lunch in thinking about the letters. She didn't know what to say.

"I meant as friends," Nathan added hastily. "I know it's too early for you to date, of course. Please don't think anything of it."

Eleanor didn't know if he was lying to make her more comfortable, or if he really did just want to be friends. Either way, she felt vaguely annoyed.

"I probably shouldn't," she said, praying he wouldn't ask her why, since there was no reason if it was really just a friendly dinner, as he said. But she wasn't to be let off the hook that easily.

"Why?"

Eleanor realized the hopelessness of her situation. She couldn't honestly say that she didn't want to, because part of her did, although part of her desperately didn't. "I don't know, Nathan. Don't ask me now." Nathan had an ironic look on his face, as if this answer was just what he had expected. "Oh all right," she found herself saying. "But not for a while. In a few weeks maybe."

It wasn't much of an acceptance, but Nathan

felt good about it anyway. He would have insisted if she hadn't given in. *It's good for her*, he told himself. *She needs to get out. With friends.* Over the past week he had convinced himself that they could never be more than friends, so it was with perfect conviction that he told himself he was doing this only for her.

Back at the cottage that evening, there was an awkward moment when Eleanor announced that she was going to bed, and Peter knew she was going upstairs to read one of the letters. But he let it go, and told her, grinning, to have fun and he'd see her in the morning. Peter had decided, although he was dying of curiosity, that he couldn't be offended if his mother didn't want to share her new interest, since he had been wishing for months that she would develop one.

Eleanor, on her part, was relieved not to feel she was sneaking around anymore. She went upstairs happily, and decided to snuggle down into bed before unfolding the next letter to read.

December 25, 1887

Winton House, Ealing

Dear Lizzie:

Merry Christmas and all my love to you, and William, and Ida and Frank! Could anything be more glorious than a Sunday Christmas? We have just returned from church up the street, an Anglican church, and far more richly decorated than our little Unitarian church back home. But, oh Lizzie, I felt like basking in religious splendor, for I felt like an angel myself! Because... last night Will gave me an engagement ring! It is a beautiful white diamond on a gold band. I am staring at it as I write this. I am so blessed to be his future wife! Could anything be more perfect than a Christmas engagement?!

I must have blushed like crazy when I opened the box. Everyone was staring and smiling at me; poor Mama burst into tears and Nellie ran up to hug me before I could even tell Will that I accepted! Then I blurted out "Yes, yes, I will be your wife..." and he came over and kissed me and everyone cheered! And then the rest of the evening seemed to be a blur, I could not help stealing glances at the ring every few minutes and asking myself if it was real or a dream. Will never left my side the whole evening. Oh Lizzie, I am so happy, and my only regret is that you are not here to share this with me.

Now I must go back and fill you in on all of the details about Ealing. We arrived on Friday and the trip was very pleasant, through charming countryside, and long but uneventful. Col. Wilkinson and his wife are delightful. They have welcomed us with open arms and made us feel quite at home. Hugh is so nice - do you remember his coming to Annisquam a few summers ago? He remembered me, or said he did, which is just as nice, and I think I remember him a little, but you know there are always so many artists with Will every summer that it is hard to remember them all. There are four other brothers! Two are unmarried, and I suspect that Will thought it would be pleasant company for Nellie, but she, as usual, seems oblivious to any possibilities of romance. The single brothers themselves are rather the shy, quiet types, so I suspect Will's efforts will end up being all for naught. The other two brothers have nice wives, but they are in and out with their families, while the only other female in residence here is their cousin Eleanor, who is a great favorite of the family, and much fun to be with. She plays and sings beautifully, and we make her entertain us every evening.

I must tell you about the house, it is so elegant! It is a huge home, in yellow brick, across from a lovely park with meadows and ponds. There is a large lawn out back, perfect for croquet, and if the weather is nice tomorrow we intend to play. Inside the house is decorated in rich, deep hues - plums and cherries - just the way I like it, and there is a crystal chandelier in the hall, and the largest Christmas tree I have ever seen in the drawing room. They have all kinds of help - maids of I don't know what type always seem to be available for whatever we need - and they have an Indian cook who puts the French version to shame, I'm sure, although the Wilkinsons say they had a terrible time teaching him to make Yorkshire pudding! There are lots of exotic artifacts from the Colonel's travels; some of them, in fact, were lent for the Science & Art Exhibition here in town last week - he lent a paddle from Samoa, a silver gilt sword from India, and a carved Maori box from New Zealand. Oh, and Lizzie, you should see the rugs, so colorful and interesting! The Wilkinson's gave Will a _real_ bear rug for Christmas, it has claws and teeth and is incredibly soft. It came from Manchuria!

The village of Ealing is just a block away, and everything we could need is within walking distance - the grocer, the florist, and bootmakers, tailors and milliners, and Mr. Fraser's gown store which has the most beautiful things! Mrs. Wilkinson and Eleanor have suggested that I pick up a few things there next week, for there will be after-Christmas sales and apparently one can never have enough gowns for London. Speaking of which, we will go up to London on Saturday, January 14. But I will write again before then.

I know Mama is writing as well today, and I can only imagine what she will say, as she is so happy for me! I'm sure she is relieved to have her youngest child married off at last, especially as I have so often tried her patience with my antics! Yet, I must say Lizzie that I feel awfully older suddenly, as if a whole new life is just beginning and I am a whole new person! Did you feel that way when you got engaged to William? I think I can picture myself as a respectable matron now, and not shudder at the thought.

Well, good-bye for now my dear, dear sister. Merry, Merry Christmas!

Love always,

Gertrude

Eleanor smiled to herself. So now they were officially engaged! It was interesting that there had once been another "Eleanor" to witness the event. *I wonder what the wedding will be like*, thought Eleanor sleepily, *although I don't suppose she'll have to write to Lizzie about that, as Lizzie will undoubtedly be taking part in it.*

The last thing Eleanor thought about before she drifted off to sleep was her own engagement party. The engagement moment itself had not been a surprise in the way Gertrude's had been - Bill had asked her to marry him one evening, and they had gone shopping together for the ring, because Bill wanted to make sure she would like it. But the party had been lovely. Eleanor remembered feeling older that night too, just as Gertrude had. After all those months of looking up to Bill, she had finally felt his equal, as if she deserved the great honor being bestowed upon her. *If only the feeling had sustained itself*, she realized. There had been many times in the years afterwards when Eleanor had felt unworthy of being Bill's wife; in fact, it seemed to her in retrospect, as the years went on she became more and more insecure, instead of more and more secure. So that when he died, she was perhaps less prepared to live on her own, than she'd been only a decade or so earlier.

It puzzled and upset Eleanor to realize this. And she was unsure why it was true. Then Grace's words from the other day came back to her: *You are afraid, Eleanor.* Had she been afraid even when she had been married? What was she afraid of?

Eleanor tossed and turned that night, trying to make sense of herself, but to her relief she did not cry. Instead, she realized that she wanted to understand herself better. She was tired of being the way she was. She wanted to change.

Eleanor suddenly realized why the letters were so important to her. She had the notion that somewhere in Gertrude's story was the answer to her own.

And yet, of course, that was ridiculous.

* * * *

Eleanor woke the next morning with a burning desire to see Grace again. She waited until 11:00, the earliest she had decided she could disturb her, and wandered down the hill to her house. She rang the doorbell, but to her distress, Grace wasn't home. As she walked slowly back up the street towards home, she was suddenly startled by the ring of a bicycle bell behind her. She turned to see Gabby just three feet away and out of breath.

"Hey stranger, I saw you from down the street and had to pedal like crazy to catch you," she announced. Eleanor loved the way she acted as if they were old friends. "What's up? Are we still on for tomorrow?"

"Definitely," Eleanor replied. "I'm more curious than ever."

"Did you find out anything new?"

Eleanor brought Gabby up to date on the latest letters. "I guess they don't shed any light on why I have them, but the more I read them, the more interesting they become."

"So, what are you doing right now?" Gabby asked.

"Nothing really. I was going to visit Grace Pippin, but she's not in."

"One of her nephews came and took her to a doctor's appointment. They waved to me in the car as they went past, just a few minutes ago. You just missed them."

"Oh. Well, I guess I'll catch up with her later."

"Do you have a bike? I was going to ride up to the Richdale market, just for the hell of it. Want to come?"

"Okay," Eleanor answered, although it was not like her to do something so spontaneous. "There's a bike in the garage. Come up the hill with me and I'll get it."

Eleanor brought Gabby to the garage behind

her cottage, and when she opened the garage door Gabby immediately noticed the truck. "Hey, whose is that?" she asked.

"Bill's," Eleanor answered.

"What year is it?"

"Nineteen seventy-five. Bill bought it when he got out of grad school."

"Does it run?"

"Oh, yeah, it runs great. I let the guys who take care of the lawn here drive it. We have a deal that they can use it for work whenever they need it, as long as they take care of it."

"Don't you ever drive it?" Gabby asked.

"No, I don't know how. It's a stick shift."

"Gee, didn't you ever want to learn? It's a nice truck!"

"No, not really." The conversation was beginning to disturb Eleanor, so she pulled out her bicycle and changed the subject. "Come on, I'll race you down the hill!"

As Eleanor and Gabby pedaled down Leonard Street, Eleanor remembered Gertrude's letter about riding the bicycle, and she was filled with a sense of wonder that she was re-tracing Gertrude's steps, over one hundred years later. "Gertrude was one of the first girls ever to ride a bicycle in Annisquam!" she called out to Gabby, and Gabby looked over to see a grin a mile wide on Eleanor's face.

By the time they reached the store, they were both ready for a break. Gabby bought a diet soda and an oatmeal creme bar; Eleanor picked up a bottle of iced tea.

"Look at this," Gabby complained, "three hundred calories in this one snack. Well, I guess that's lunch."

"You can't be on a diet," Eleanor commented, observing Gabby's slim frame.

"Oh, no, I'm not, but I do watch calories. Slimness doesn't run in my family, you know!"

Eleanor laughed. Tom Newsome, Gabby's father, was a short, rotund man who looked absolutely nothing like Gabby. "You must take after your mother," Eleanor observed.

"I hope so, my Mom's beautiful. She's back in France this summer, visiting her family. I was invited, of course, but I love working at the Historical Society too much to miss a summer. In fact," she added, looking at her watch, "I have to man the shop again this afternoon. You should come too; we hardly brushed the surface the other night."

Eleanor agreed, and they rode back into town. Eleanor swung up to the cottage to get the photograph she'd copied, and met Gabby back at the Historical Society.

"Let's look through the rest of these photographs and see what else we can find," Gabby suggested.

There were a number of photographs of artists painting on the beaches of Annisquam, and often the people were identified on the reverse. There were plenty of pictures that included William Lamb Picknell and "Gertrude Picknell," so Eleanor knew they had been taken after their marriage. Then they came upon an envelope labeled "Langdon family." Inside were a number of photographs, almost all unidentified, and very few seemed to have been taken in Annisquam. However, Eleanor could pick out Gertrude, Lizzie, Ida and Frank in a number of them, as well as the young lady that Eleanor had decided could be Katherine Langdon. A bell went off in her head.

"It just occurred to me why "Katherine Langdon" wasn't identified on the other photograph. That photo must have been a present from Ida to Katherine - which would make her identification unnecessary - and the photo must have originally come to you with the others in this envelope."

"That's very likely. Things are always being taken out of their proper places and then misfiled back," Gabby noted.

"Were these photographs a present to the Historical Society from the Langdon family?" Eleanor asked.

"I don't know. I'll have to ask my Dad. But it seems as if someone in their family must have left them to us."

Eleanor suddenly wondered if there were living descendants of the Langdons, Picknells or Johnsons. And it occurred to her that if there were, she should try to get the letters to them eventually. She was about to mention this to Gabby, when the younger woman suddenly exclaimed, "I wonder where this was taken? It looks just like my mother's part of France!"

Gabby was looking at a photograph taken in a tropical garden. In the center, in front of a palm tree, stood Gertrude, and she was holding a child. She looked elegant, in a soft dark dress with black trim, and she was smiling at the one or two-year old child, who was wearing a white smock and frilly bonnet, and was frowning at the camera. "Boy or girl, do you think?" Eleanor asked Gabby.

"Oh, boy, definitely, you can tell by the hair. They wore those types of outfits until they were about six, back in those days. But look at the scenery - I could swear that was the south of France!"

Eleanor was less interested in the landscape than the child. Was it Gertrude's son? Gertrude and William's? Or just a neighbor or relative? Her thoughts were interrupted by Gabby, who was asking her if she wanted to copy this photograph as well.

"No..." Eleanor replied slowly. "Let me read more letters, and see if this is her child, or someone else's, first."

Yet, deep down, Eleanor felt she knew. It made perfect sense to her that Gertrude would have had a son, because she, Eleanor, had a son. There was too much coincidence between their lives for this not to be the case.

Eleanor and Gabby looked through a few more files, but didn't turn up anything else. They agreed to meet in front of the Historical Society at ten the next morning, and head off to Salem. As she pedaled home, Eleanor kept thinking about Gertrude's son, and wondering if he grew up to have any children, and if they might still be alive, somewhere.

She remembered to stop at Grace's house, although she was so distracted by the thought of Gertrude's child, that she couldn't quite remember what she had been so anxious to see Grace about. Grace was in her garden, and Eleanor helped her pick weeds while she gathered her thoughts together and tried to recall what she wanted to talk with her about. It was Grace who ultimately reminded her.

"How are your 'small steps' coming along?" she abruptly asked. "Have you been feeling any better about things?"

"I realized something disturbing last night,"

Eleanor told her. "I think I might have been scared, like we talked about, even when I was married. And I don't know why."

"Well, I'm no psychologist," Grace began, "but it seems to me these things often go back to childhood. What kind of an upbringing did you have?"

Eleanor shuddered at the thought of recounting the whole story of her family, and the secret of her sister's death, but she managed to vocalize the main gist of the matter. "They were a bit strange," she admitted. "They weren't very good at facing problems."

"Then perhaps that's the root of it," Grace commented. "It can be very difficult to know how to face life yourself, if your own parents weren't a good role model. But one thing I'm sure of, Ellie, it's never too late to learn. Don't let the past become a crutch - you go out there and face life head on. You'll soon become good at it, trust me."

"You always sound so sure about me, Grace. Far more sure than I feel about myself."

"We all need a cheering squad, Ellie. That will be my job. You just stop by and see me whenever you're having a hard time coping, and I'll set you back on the right path!"

They chatted a while longer, and Grace reminded Eleanor that Miranda's youngest daughter, Kelly, would be arriving with her family on the weekend. Eleanor promised to visit them as soon as they were settled.

Before going home, Eleanor decided to turn up Walnut Street and see what Nathan and Peter were doing with the Conboy house. As she biked up the drive she saw Peter on a ladder, carefully scraping trim up at the roofline. Nathan had one eye on him from below, and was giving him advice that mainly consisted of "Be careful;" while with his other eye Nathan was spackling some trim on the corner of the house.

"Ellie!" he called out as soon as she was within sight. "Come to see us slaving away, eh?"

"Yes, I've come to see how you're spending your summer vacation," Eleanor replied good-naturedly. "You've certainly done a job on that house. It looks like it has leprosy."

"Nathan is making me scrape every inch of it. The poor thing is going to look a lot worse before it gets better," Peter said.

"Peter, Grace Pippin just reminded me that the Smiths are coming this weekend. Alan will be looking forward to seeing you."

Nathan looked concerned. "Peter, I hate to keep you away from your friends all summer. You know, you don't have to work five days a week if you don't want to. We could cut back your hours."

"Oh, no, I like this. And I need the money. I can see Alan after supper and on the weekends."

"Okay, but if you change your mind, don't hesitate to mention it." Nathan was pleased that Peter enjoyed the work, and his company, enough to give up his playtime.

"What do you need the money for?" Eleanor asked Peter, out of curiosity.

"I'm saving up for a car when I'm sixteen," he promptly replied.

"Well, that's ambitious. Do all your friends have cars on their minds already?"

"Most of my friends don't realize yet that you have to plan for things in advance. They think everything will always be the same. Easy. They haven't had to think about life much yet."

This small speech said a world about Peter's maturity, but also a world about the circumstances that had created it. Eleanor felt uncomfortable, and looked down at the driveway. She kicked some small pebbles with her toe. Nathan broke the awkward moment.

"So what kind of car, if you had all the money in the world, would you want, Peter?"

"A 1964 Ford Mustang. White, with leather interior. But I'll settle for anything that runs when the time comes. Just give me a set of wheels so I can hit the open road..." he sang. Peter was only having fun, but for a painful moment Eleanor was reminded of her brothers, and their flight from home as soon as possible. Did Peter feel the same way? Was home an intolerable place?

Before she'd even thought it through, Eleanor found herself saying, "You can have your father's pickup truck if you'd like."

Peter's eyes got wide, and he broke into a huge grin. "Really? I love that truck! Can I really have it? I thought you hated it."

"Why did you think that?"

"I don't know. You've always seemed funny about it."

"It's just that I can't drive it," she said to Nathan, as a way of explanation.

"Why not?" Nathan asked.

"I don't know how to drive a stick shift. I never learned."

"Well, it's never too late. You can't teach Peter how to drive it unless you know how yourself, you know."

Until that moment Eleanor had never

considered the fact that she was the one who would have to teach Peter to drive. She had always assumed that was something Bill and Peter would do together. Now it would be up to her. But the last thing on earth she wanted to do was learn how to drive that truck, especially when she had resisted it for all those years with Bill. *Oh, well, perhaps he'll forget about it by the time he's sixteen*, she thought to herself, although she knew perfectly well that would never happen.

"I'd be happy to teach you," Nathan was continuing.

"That's okay. There's no rush. After all, I've still got two years."

"Less," Peter pointed out. "I'm almost fourteen-and-a half, remember?"

"Yes, of course." Eleanor wanted to change the subject. "So when do you two think Mrs. Conboy's house will be finished?"

"Oh, another two weeks, I'd say," Nathan answered for both of them. "We're almost ready to paint. This is the hard part. The painting will be easy."

"This has been a lot harder than I'd expected," Peter admitted. "But it's fun. I like it."

"Well, I'll leave you two alone now. See you at dinner, Peter," Eleanor said as she turned to go.

"Hey, Ellie, let me know how it goes in Salem tomorrow!" Nathan called after her, and Eleanor waved in response.

* * * *

By the time she got home she had just enough time to read another letter, before she had to start dinner.

January 14, 1888

Dear Lizzie,

I know I have been remiss in not writing sooner. Here we are on the train to London and I kept promising myself I would write everyday, but somehow there was always something to keep me from doing it. Well, enough excuses! I'm sure you are hardly waiting by the mailbox for my letters!

As you undoubtedly suspect, I am having a wonderful, fabulous, incredible time! This past week we have been so busy. The weather has been fine and we've had many games of croquet and lawn tennis. Having so many Wilkinson brothers around made it particularly fun. There was very much laughing and very little serious competition, although, you know me, I can never play at anything without wanting to win.

I actually miss them all already, and we've only been on the train an hour. I think I've made a friend of Eleanor for life...

(Yes, you have, the modern Eleanor thought to herself with a smile.)

...and I do hope she'll come to the States to visit us sometime.

Tuesday night we went to the Lyric Hall to see the tableaux vivant. Oh, Lizzie, it was so much fun! There were about forty sets. They did a thrilling version of "The Last Days of Pompeii," with a real fire-spouting volcano!

But by far the funniest scene was "Mr. Pickwick in the Ladies' School." The audience laughed so hard that the actors almost broke character, and they had to delay the next scene until the audience and performers had recovered themselves!

On Thursday, Will took me to Haven Green Chapel to hear Miss Von Finkelstein's lecture on "The Bedouins of the Desert." He is particularly interested in everything Oriental. It was a very enlightening experience for me - I really had no idea what life in the desert was like for the natives, especially the women. I was surprised to discover that Bedouin women take a great part in public policies and affairs. Of course, that is how it should be, but Miss Von Finkelstein seems to think that Bedouin women, in that regard at least, have it better than we Westerners. In their own culture, one could say that they have the vote. Perhaps you can use that information at your next women's rights meeting!

This is a very nice, comfortable train. It's a new service from Ealing that just commenced at the beginning of the month. Nellie just got up to get us some refreshments from the dining car. While she is away I will quickly write that as I had expected, none of the Wilkinson brothers caught her fancy. I believe she is a confirmed maiden! However, I am too selfish to be disappointed; perhaps she and Minnie will come and live with us often - - that would be splendid!

Mama says that if I don't put in that she sends her love she will be very angry! As if I wouldn't say so! I know she writes to you more than I do, the dear. She is having a wonderful time, Lizzie. It is so good to see! I think it is the best time she's had since Papa died.

I am so excited about seeing London. I have so many plans! I want to see everything! Will's friends in

London have reserved some nice rooms for us near Hyde Park. I shall tell you all about them in my next letter. Will is going to be staying nearby, with a portrait painter, Frank Brooks.

Good-bye for now, and love to all, especially Frank and Ida. I do miss them so much! But I have discovered that I love to travel, Lizzie. Now that I have discovered this I suspect I'll be wanting to plan trips constantly!

Ever, ever your loving sister,

Gertrude

As Eleanor broiled some fish filets and tossed together a salad, she thought about Gertrude's world and the treasure trove of historical information contained in the letters. *Tableaux vivant...* she knew what they were but she'd never seen one, of course. How much fun they must have been! She imagined baseball and bicycles being new; not having the vote; lectures on Bedouin women... *Yes,* she thought decisively, *I really must get these letters to a descendant at some point. Someone is missing out on an awful lot of family history.*

Again she wondered about Gertrude's son, and almost unconsciously she found herself contemplating her own son, Peter, in a different light. If Peter was the modern-day equivalent of Gertrude's son, in some cosmic way, then he was part of the puzzle too. She vowed to pay more attention to him, not to be as caught up in her own world all the time.

All that evening Peter was the happy recipient of Eleanor's re-ignited interest in him. For the first time in two years, Peter felt that he was getting his mother back.

6

Eleanor was waiting outside the Historical Society promptly at ten a.m. Gabby pulled up in a white Probe, just the kind of sporty-but-not-too-flashy car Eleanor expected her to own. On the drive to Salem, Gabby explained how the title search would work.

"We have to start with a date when we know the deed was changed. Was there a deed change when you acquired the cottage from Bill's parents?" she asked.

"I believe so," Eleanor replied. "That was eight years ago."

"Great! You'll be amazed at how easy the whole thing is, once you get going."

They pulled up in front of a large grey building, next to the courthouse. To Eleanor's surprise, they had to go through a metal detector, and let their bags be examined, before they were allowed into the Land Records building. The entrance hallway emptied into a great room, stacked floor to ceiling with shelves of records. All around the room people were pulling large books off of shelves and riffling through the pages at counters. A few of these researchers seemed to have obtained their own permanent, but makeshift, desks.

"Professional title researchers," Gabby explained. "They do so much work here they set up shop."

"Okay," she began, as she led Eleanor to a row of books marked by date in the center of the room. "We need 1989. Ah, here it is. Let's see what it says about your deed."

They quickly found the right page. "See this number at the bottom?" Gabby pointed out. "That's the first clue in the treasure hunt. We have to find the book with that number, and then that page. That's the reference for the previous deed, and that will tell us whom Ben and Mary got the cottage from."

They wandered through the shelves at the front of the room until they found number 3261. On page 228 they found the deed, giving ownership of the property from Mary's parents, the Stuarts, to Ben and Mary, in 1947.

"That was the year they were married. It must have been a wedding present," Eleanor told Gabby.

"Nice!" Gabby exclaimed. "Hey, maybe I can get my Dad to hand over our cottage to me when *I* tie the knot!" she added.

Gabby quickly ran her eyes over the page. "Here's the next reference. Book 2543, page 66."

Eleanor brought the next book over, and turned to page sixty-six. "Okay. This is when Bill's great-grandparents left the cottage to the Stuarts. Elijah and Anne Stuart deeded the cottage to Seward and Marion Stuart, in June of 1920. Mary, Bill's mother, was born in 1926 - six years after they inherited the cottage."

"Go get the next one," Gabby said. "Book 2198, page 144."

Eleanor ran to track down the next volume, and brought it over to Gabby. Together they found the right page.

"This is a sale from Johnathan Flagg to Elijah and Anne Stuart in September of 1905."

"Who's Johnathan Flagg?" Gabby asked.

"I don't know. I'll have to ask Mary." Eleanor wrote the information down.

"The next reference is book 1856. You go get it while I read this carefully to see if there's any clue about Mr. Flagg in it."

Eleanor retrieved the next book, and upon returning Gabby told her, "There's really nothing here about Johnathan Flagg, except that once he's referred to as 'Dr. Flagg.' He must have been a doctor of some kind."

Eleanor turned to the appropriate page in the next volume. "This is interesting. Johnathan Flagg only owned the property for two years. He bought it from John Hall in January of 1903. And look, there's a map!" she added excitedly.

"Yes, that's your property," Gabby agreed, but to Eleanor's surprise, she was frowning.

"What's wrong?" Eleanor asked.

"Look - the map doesn't have any house on it. I just realized that there's no way of telling from this title search when the cottage was moved from the Point to your property. I forgot - title searches only trace the *land* history, not the history of buildings."

"Would the cottage be on the map if it was there in 1903?" Eleanor asked.

"Yes."

"Then don't we know that the cottage had to have been moved *after* 1903?"

"Yes, but we don't know if Johnathan Flagg moved it, or the Stuarts. That means that it could have been moved anytime between 1903 and, well, when did you say Mary was born?"

"1926."

"Well, the cottage must have been there when Mary was born, don't you think, or she would remember something about it?" Gabby conjectured.

"I haven't properly asked her, but she's always referred to it as if it has been there forever, so I doubt she knows anything about it being moved. I'll call her in Florida tonight and see what she says."

"Okay. Let's go back one more reference and see what happens."

The next deed revealed that the Hall family had owned the land for over forty years.

"I bet they were farmers. It was probably just pasture back then," Gabby noted. "I'm going to go ask the clerks if they have any suggestions about finding out when the cottage was moved. You put these books away and I'll meet you back here in a few minutes."

Gabby pushed through the glass doors at the end of the room and disappeared into an office. After a while she came back, with a funny smile on her face.

"Well, I've got good news and bad news. The good news is that there is a way to find out, maybe. The bad news is that it's extremely difficult."

"Well, spit it out, I'm all in suspense."

"It seems there are two possible ways of figuring it out. One is to look at the tax assessments on the property for each year and find out when the property taxes go up. That would be the easiest way except for one problem - the tax assessor won't let you look through the old records yourself, and the staff is usually too busy to do it for you. You'd have to put in a request in writing and hope to get an answer before you leave in the fall."

"Oh. What's the second way?"

Gabby grinned. "Go to the Gloucester Archives and look at City Council records for each year, looking for a record of the cottage being moved. There might be one, there might not.

"That doesn't sound so bad. Why are you grinning?"

"Wait till you see those records. Each book weighs 100 pounds, I swear. And they are very particular in the Archives. They have very limited hours and they only help two people at a time, and bring out one piece of material at a time, that sort of thing. You'll have to charm them, Eleanor, if you expect to find out anything before Christmas!"

Seeing Eleanor's glum face, Gabby continued teasingly. "Don't look so downtrodden! You could charm them if anyone could."

"Oh, I don't know about that. But I suppose I'll have to try."

"Well, maybe you won't. If Bill's mom can tell you anything definite, perhaps you won't need to go to the Archives at all."

"That's true. Perhaps this deed information will jog her memory. After all, I never really discussed the matter with her. It's always just been casual conversation about family history."

"Right," Gabby said with encouragement. "You never know what people will remember when it's necessary."

Eleanor suddenly laughed at herself. "Yes, but really, Gabby, is any of this *necessary*? I'm realizing more and more that it's just my insatiable curiosity that wants to know."

"I think a desk in the attic with mysterious letters is very interesting, and I would be dying of curiosity too if it happened to me," Gabby assured her.

Gabby quickly took care of her own business in the building, and then the two women gathered up their belongings and left, both noting that they were remarkably hungry. They re-fed the meter, and walked up a few blocks until they found a cheerful-looking sandwich shop. "Please let me buy your lunch," Eleanor insisted. "I could never have done this without you, and I really want to thank you properly."

"I won't put up a fight!" Gabby laughed. "I'm only a poor student, and can't look gift horses in the mouth!"

"Oh, do you go to school?" Eleanor asked, as they sat down and began perusing the menu.

"I start graduate school in History next fall."

"History! Why am I not surprised?" Eleanor smiled at the younger woman. "I can tell how much you love it."

"Oh, I do! It's my father's greatest gift to me, don't you think? I mean - he was kind enough to let me inherit the 'looks' genes from my mother, but he sure passed on his love of history to me!"

"Well, you'll do great. What do you want to do with it someday? Teach? Write?"

"I don't know. I'd love to do both. Anyway, I'll have to publish if I want to teach at a college level, won't I?"

"Yes. There's no getting around it nowadays."

After they'd ordered sandwiches, Eleanor told Gabby a little bit about Bill's career, and what she knew about university teaching positions.

"Do *you* teach?" Gabby asked.

"No. Whatever made you think that?"

"I figured that if you had a career, it had to be one that allowed you to take the summer off. Teaching seemed like a natural. Of course, there are others."

"Yes. Like homemaker."

Gabby regarded Eleanor with interest. "Now don't take this the wrong way. I have great respect for homemakers. After all, my mother is one, and I've loved having her around all the time. But you just seemed to me like a person with a career. You're so bright and all. And you always have interesting things to talk about besides your home and family. So I thought you must have a career."

"Well, that's too flattering for me to take offense, I guess. But until Bill died, it really seemed like a full-time job just taking care of the family. Bill worked at home a lot, you know, so I felt like a part of his career. I was always there to make him comfortable, to be a sounding board for his ideas, to act as his gatekeeper and fan-mail reader, that sort of thing. Plus, being a mother is very time-consuming, especially before your children head off to school. But now, I don't know. I don't know what I would do now if I did decide to take up a career."

"What did you major in in college?" Gabby asked.

"Writing. I was a writer too."

Gabby's eyes narrowed. "Now, Eleanor, what do you mean by 'I *was* a writer?' I thought writing was like being a poet, or a philosopher." She continued with vehemence. "You either are one, or you're not. It's either in your blood, or you don't have it. It's inside you - it's what you *are*, not what you do!"

"I don't understand your point."

"Sure you do," Gabby insisted firmly. "If you are a writer, then you should write. If you never write, well, it's not even worth mentioning that you once fancied you would, is it?"

Eleanor was struck by Gabby's attitude. It made her feel strangely ashamed, but also elated. *Was* she a writer? "I don't know what to say," she told the younger woman.

"Just think about it. If I'm right, and I think I am, then it will all come clear to you if you only think about it," she said with utter assurance. "If you are a writer, than deep down inside you, you know you are. And you'll have to write, that's all there is to it."

The sandwiches arrived and momentarily broke off the conversation. Then Gabby resumed. "Have you really not written anything in all the years you've been out of school?"

"I'm ashamed to admit it, but yes. I couldn't compete with Bill. It wouldn't have been healthy for me to try, for us, for our relationship, I mean."

"Why? Look at Barrett and Browning! They were both successful, and they admired each other tremendously!"

"Yes, but I don't have that kind of temperament. Or maybe I don't have that kind of faith in myself."

"Did Bill think you were a good writer?"

"I don't know. Maybe. He said I was when I was his student. I guess he did."

"Didn't he try to get you to write after you were married?"

"No. Well, he did, I guess. I didn't pay any attention to it, though."

Gabby sat back and paused, her sandwich poised

in midair, and seemed to regard Eleanor as if for the first time. "Eleanor Strayer, you are your own worst enemy, aren't you?" she suddenly announced.

Eleanor burst out laughing. "You certainly have a way of making me feel so!"

"Well, *I* think you're a writer. I can just tell. It's the way you've grabbed on to this Gertrude thing. Your mind is on fire, and you won't rest until you've satisfied yourself that you've figured out the whole story. Just wait - you'll have to write about it, sooner or later."

It had been so long since Eleanor had thought of herself as anything but Bill's wife, that Gabby's comments gave her the strange sensation that her outside did not match her inside - that the way she appeared to everyone else was not the way she felt about herself. She wondered that Gabby could have a strong sense of her at all after only a few meetings, and then be so adamant about it. Perhaps that was just Gabby's way. Anyway, she had no intention of becoming a writer. Not at this late date.

For the rest of the meal, and the drive home, Eleanor kept the conversation firmly centered on Gabby instead of herself, and the time flew by. When she arrived home, she immediately telephoned Mary in Florida.

Her mother-in-law was delighted to hear from her. "Ellie! I was hoping you'd call. I've been wondering how your summer is going."

"Well, it's turning out to be more interesting than I'd expected. I have a bunch of questions to ask you, but first I must apologize for not bringing this up last week when you called. Chalk it up to a perverse sense of secrecy. Are you ready?"

"Well, I'm dying of curiosity, now! What in the world do you want to ask me?"

"When we first got to the cottage I went up to the attic to get the window screens, and in that huge desk up there I found a packet of letters. Letters from a Gertrude Powers to her sister Lizzie Johnson. Remember I asked you about Lizzie?"

"Yes. I still don't know who she is."

"Well, Gertrude and Lizzie's family apparently rented this cottage in the summers back in the 1880s. The cottage was located on Pleasure Point then. Do you know anything about that?"

"Goodness, no. I thought the cottage had always been on Planter's Neck. Are you sure you have the right cottage?"

"Yes, there's really no doubt about it. Not only is this cottage, and the twin next door, pictured in old photographs taken on the Point, but there's no other way to account for the letters being here, is there?"

"So you are saying that both cottages were moved up to Planter's Neck a long time ago."

"I guess so. But you don't remember your parents ever mentioning anything about it?"

"No, dear. I really believe they inherited the land with the cottage."

"Well, if you are right, then the cottage was moved here by your grandparents, or by a Johnathan Flagg, who owned the land before your grandparents."

"Really? How do you know that?"

"Gabby Newsome took me down to Salem and we did a title search. When this Dr. Flagg bought the land in 1903, it didn't have a cottage on it. But he sold it to your grandparents in 1905. Which means the cottage must have been moved between 1903 and 1920, when your parents inherited it."

"I suspect so, Ellie. I really believe Mom and Dad would have mentioned it if they had moved the cottage themselves. Still, I can't be sure. It might have been moved before I was born, and they just never thought to tell me."

"Hmmm..." Ellie pondered this information. "I don't suppose you've ever heard of this Dr. Flagg before?"

"No. It's too bad Mom and Dad are no longer with us. I wonder what they would say about the whole thing."

"Me too."

"But Ellie, I'm still confused. Even if the cottage was moved, why do you think the letters are there?"

"I can't figure that out. Maybe it will come clear to me by the time I finish reading all the letters."

"Goodness, Ellie, are there hundreds of them?!"

"No, Mom, I'm just a slow reader. No, I'm kidding. I'm only reading one a day. It's somehow more fun that way." Eleanor didn't think there was any point in mentioning to Mary that she dreaded reading the last letter, and was putting it off as long as possible.

"Well, if you find out anything else, give me a call. I'm full of curiosity now. By the way, the desk has always been there, at least as long as I can remember. I once asked Dad how it got up in the attic, because you can see that it won't fit through the current doorway. He told me they completely renovated the cottage when I was a baby, so they could live there year-round. It used to have no insulation, you know, just being a summer place. Anyway, they had to close off the attic to retain heat. The desk was up there, and they just left it. Now that I think about it, he might have even said that it came with the cottage."

"It must have, really, to have Gertrude's letters."

"Yes, I can see that. It certainly is odd that we never found the letters before this. I would have sworn I'd looked in that desk myself and found it empty."

"They may have been stuck behind the bottom drawer. The drawer fell down and that's when I noticed them. So maybe they were always there, hidden."

"Well, they certainly are making your summer interesting. What else is going on?"

Eleanor filled Mary in on Peter and Nathan's progress on the Conboy house, and mentioned the sailing trip to Newburyport. She left out the dinner invitation, however. Then she talked about Gabby, and Grace, and the coming arrival of Miranda's daughter's family.

"I haven't seen Kelly in ages," Eleanor realized. "Bill always liked her so much."

"Oh yes, she was his favorite baby-sitter when they were children! Kelly always was a sweet child."

"Well, her youngest son Alan is a great favorite of Peter's. He really missed seeing him last year."

"He'll have to make up for lost time. How long are the Smiths staying?"

"Oh, I don't know. A week or two I think."

"Well, say Hi to them for us, and to Miranda of course. And give Grace our love. She's a character, isn't she?!"

"She's one of my favorite people. She has a way

about her that's very comforting."

"I'm not surprised. Having all that family around her over the years has made her very wise."

"Oh, you haven't done so badly yourself!" Eleanor quickly offered.

"Thank you, dear. Now I'd better go and start supper. Talk to you soon!"

"Bye, Mom."

But only two minutes later the phone rang, and it was Mary again. To Eleanor's surprise, she was crying.

"Ellie, I just had to call back and tell you how happy I am! That's the first conversation I've had with you since the funeral where you actually sounded, well, happy!"

Eleanor burst into tears herself. "I think I am a little bit happy! Oh, Mom, why are we crying? This is ridiculous!"

"I don't know. It's just such a relief. Ellie, I was beginning to think you'd never be yourself again."

"Mom, I don't even know who 'myself' is. But thank you. I think maybe I am feeling better about life. I want to, I know."

"Bill would want you to, Ellie. Don't ever forget that. I think that's the one lesson you've been unable to accept."

"I know." Eleanor was solemn. "I just feel so bad about being happy, still. I miss him so much!"

"I do too, dear. But you can't stop living yourself because your husband has passed away. You're on the right track now, Ellie. You just stay there and don't look back."

Eleanor promised that she would try. She felt less confident about her new-found interest in life than

Mary did, but she was ready to hope that it might be permanent. She was tired, achingly tired, of being sad.

* * * *

Later that evening, Eleanor read Gertrude's next letter. It was written from London, with a return address of 24 Ennismore Gardens, SW.

January 19, 1888

Dear Lizzie:

We are all settled in our London flat. Mama and I are on the second floor, with two bedrooms, a large sunny sitting room, and a large bathroom with a lavatory and water closet. It is quite luxurious! Nellie and Mrs. Picknell are one floor below us, and the landlady, Mrs. Winters, lives upstairs. It is such a lovely spot! We look out over a garden square, and Hyde Park is only a block away. We are perfectly convenient to the omnibuses, which take us everywhere. And I do mean everywhere, Lizzie - I believe we have packed more activity into these past few days than most tourists do in a month!

On Sunday it was a lovely day and I simply insisted that we go to the zoo! You know how I love animals. They have new wolves' and foxes' dens, and the animals were very active because the weather was so splendid. We had a lovely time walking around, and everyone was naturally exhausted by the end of the day, but nevertheless I dragged them all to see Madame

Tussaud's Exhibitions that evening. I was determined to go in the evening, to get the full effect of the Chamber of Horrors, and somehow I got my way although I can assure you that Mama and Mrs. Picknell were reluctance personified. How Nellie and I laughed at them, and played games with them in that Chamber! Oh, I thought they would murder us themselves, and become part of the exhibit! It was so much fun... How Frank would have loved it!

The next day it was time for Will to get serious, so we made the round of art exhibitions. First we went to Grosvenor Gallery to see the winter exhibition, "A Century of British Art." There were half-a-dozen Constables and Turners, some exquisite Boningtons, some very fine DeWints, and some interesting Richard Wilsons, lent from the British Minister in Spain. My favorite were the George Morlands, however - I prefer landscapes with figures, don't you?

Next it was off to Boussod, Valadon & Company. They had a collection of pictures from Will's French dealer, Goupil. There were works by Carolus Duran, Gerome (Will's teacher), Bastien Lepage, Daubigny, and wonderful new works by Corot. I do think the French put the English to shame when it comes to sensitivity and innovation. But I'm sure I am influenced by Will's feelings in this; he does so love the French.

Down the street there was a fascinating exhibition of Japanese crafts: pottery, metalwork, porcelain, laquer and bronzes. This was a nice change after looking at so many paintings. Now, Lizzie, you won't believe who walked into the Japanese exhibition while we were there - - the artist Whistler! He looked just exactly as you would expect - moustache, streak of silver in his hair, eyepiece in his eye, and carrying a walking stick which I half-expected he would use to strike people who annoyed him! But he turned out to be a perfect gentleman. Will and he have a nodding acquaintance, and Mr. Whistler graciously came over and introduced himself to us all, and Lizzie, I could not take my eyes off his hands - they were so slim and elegant! His fingers were in constant motion, so beautiful! They were as fascinating to watch as a butterfly - it is no wonder that he uses that as his monogram!

On Tuesday Mama and Mrs. Picknell needed to rest, and Will met some of his artist friends at the Royal Academy, so Nellie and I played the tourist, and went to Westminster Abbey, and Parliament, and Buckingham Palace to try to catch a glimpse of the Queen. Of course we did not. It was a blustery day, so we sat and had tea at a restaurant for much of the afternoon, and talked and talked. It was surprising how much we still had to talk about, after spending all these weeks together!

Yesterday we went to the matinee at the Globe Theater to see Wilson Barrett as Hamlet. Nellie had heard that it was an innovative production, and it truly was. Mr. Barrett is a very young Hamlet, which quite fits the story better than the older actors I've seen play that role at home. The play scene was done in the open air, which was a nice effect, and pleased Nellie immensely.

I should like to see the Pantomine at Drury Lane, and Hengler's Circus. And I must get to the Egyptian Hall to see the magic show and the mechanical orchestra! I love that kind of thing, and how I love to see Will laugh! He can be too serious sometimes; I do believe he needs me to keep him young!

I have to leave off writing now for Mama is getting ready to send the wash out. We had the silliest argument this morning over whether Epps's Cocoa or Schweitzer's Cocoatina is a more soothing drink! We have been *drinking chocolate every morning since we've been in England, and now have formed stubborn opinions about it!*

I do so wish you were here with us...

All my love,

Gertrude

Eleanor lay back in bed and sighed, feeling somewhat envious of Gertrude. Gertrude seemed to truly enjoy life, to a degree that Eleanor herself had never attempted. *I wish I was more like Gertrude... or Gabby*, she thought idly. *Both of them seem to know just what they are doing all the time.* Eleanor lay in bed and thought about all the things that had happened to Gertrude, and how she approached everything with enthusiasm and optimism. She forgot about Gertrude's earlier doubts about herself, or the way the last letter began. All she saw in Gertrude was someone charming, and full of life, and able to handle all the situations in which she found herself. *I'm going to try to be more like her...* she thought to herself, as she drifted off to sleep. *Perhaps that's what I'm meant to do.*

* * * *

The next few days were relatively uneventful. Eleanor went to the bookstore and picked up some summer reading in which she indulged in long, languorous days on the beach. One day she drove into Rockport and wandered through the shops and galleries, finally purchasing a light, summer handbag to replace the heavy leather one she'd been toting about. On one evening Nathan and Peter dragged her out for a pizza dinner in Gloucester, and the evening was casual and delightful - Nathan never once reminded her of her promise to have dinner with him sometime alone. And Eleanor did check into the hours of the Gloucester Archives, but decided that she could finish the letters before trying to determine if there was a record of her cottage being moved from the Point.

And every day, there were new letters to read.

24 Ennismore Gardens, S.W.
London, England

January 28, 1888

Dear Lizzie:

Tonight there was a lunar eclipse that we could have seen splendidly from our roof, but unfortunately it was too cloudy. Mama and I are sitting in our cozy little parlor writing letters. Mrs. Winters brought down some cake earlier, and we four women stuffed ourselves (actually five women, for Mrs. Winters was not adverse to joining us!), so now we are all in a stupor. But stupors make for good moods to write in, I think.

This week has been so busy! The highlight was last Tuesday evening. We went to hear the London Symphony, and we were all in ecstasy! The main performance was of Dr. F. Bridges's "Morte d'Arthur," based on the Tennyson poem. Oh it was divine! So soulful and dramatic, you could feel each movement and part of the story as it was played out. They also played Bizet's "Roma." I am not a big Bizet fan but this was quite nice. And then there was a newly discovered Mozart serenade called "Haffner." It seems as if there are endless numbers of undiscovered works coming to the forefront lately! This one was not as good as his other works, which perhaps explains why he tried to hide it!

We did go to the Egyptian Hall this week, just Will and I, and I enjoyed myself tremendously, although I fear Will thought the whole thing was silly. I love illusions, and puppets, and ventriloquists! But perhaps what I loved best was being alone with Will... do you realize we have hardly spent a minute alone together since we arrived in England?! Everyone keeps offering to leave us alone, but they never do! And we can't be such spoilsports as to go off and do fun things without them. The only reason we were alone at the Egyptian Hall was because I was the only child in the group who wanted to go!

Oh, I read that over, and it sounds as if I am complaining. No, no, dear Lizzie, I am not so silly as all that! I know what a wonderful opportunity this has been for me, and I am having a wonderful time, and I know that in the years to come Will and I will spend so much time alone together that we shall probably wish desperately for people to visit us and relieve our misery! (Oh, I hope I am only kidding!)

Back to this week's adventures. We saw a lovely exhibition of watercolors at the Royal Society of Painters in Watercolors. Nellie and I were very interested to see how our little amateur attempts compare to the masters, and I must confess that we are far from qualifying for admittance to the Society! The work was so delicate, so exact and fresh! Will was perhaps the most impressed of us all, for he understands the difficulties of the medium best, *and declared that he'd always thought the English were the finest watercolorists in the world - which is a supreme compliment, coming from him.*

We also went to a reception at the Royal Society of British Artists on Suffolk Street. Their winter exhibition closes this week, and there was a small party for artist members. It was quite lovely - we met many artists whose works we had admired previously. So many of them knew Will, and how honored I felt to be introduced as his betrothed!

Will has been so sweet to me, yet I begin to sense that he is just a little anxious for us to go. You must understand, Lizzie, that he has given up these many weeks when he would normally be in the New Forest, painting. I see that he longs to get back to work. I cannot complain, for to love him is to love him as an artist - he is that and can never be anything else. I could not be more proud of his talent, or believe more in the importance of what he does.

I am growing sleepy. I will write again before we sail.

Your loving sister,

Gertrude

February 3, 1888
24 Ennismore Gardens, S.W.
London, England

Dear Lizzie,

We are resting before the big event tonight - a

party at Frederic, Lord Leighton's home! There is to be dinner and a concert by Clara Schumann. I am so looking forward to seeing the house - Will says it is like an Oriental fantasy, with an Arab Hall and a Moorish courtyard, Turkish carpets, Greek vases and hothouse flowers everywhere! I am sure it will be divine. And the guest list includes many artists and their wives, so I shall have the chance to make acquaintances with whom I can discuss the daily life of an artist's wife. I do so want to make a good impression, and be the kind of wife that Will can be proud of!

I am going to wear a stunning blue dress that I purchased in Ealing. It shows off my blue eyes, and looks well with that red mop of mine (I still hate my hair, Lizzie). Mama says I look dazzling in it - I do hope Will thinks so as well! She is letting me borrow her diamond earrings, which is very, very sweet of her, as they are the best ones she brought, and I'm sure she should wear them herself. But she says all eyes will be on me, not on her, so I might as well look "as beautiful on the outside as I am on the inside" (those were her very words, Lizzie, I almost cried). Isn't our mother an absolute angel?!

Sunday we must leave for Liverpool, in order to make the Palmyra on Tuesday. Mama is shaken up again about sailing, because of the English steamship that was lost off the coast of China. There was a gruesome description of it in the paper, written by the third engineer, who I believe was the only survivor. I keep reassuring her. Personally I am more worried about seasickness than drowning. Some people here have recommended Beecham's Pills - - I'll let you know if they work!

Oh, I must run and get dressed but first I must tell you one funny thing. We went to see the Bicycle and

*Tricycle show at the Royal Aquarium. It was a huge
exhibition - over 140 stands - and there was every type of
bicycle that you could imagine! The most unique, I think,
was called a road-sculler. It was half tricycle and half
rowing machine! But the best part, Lizzie, is that they
were showing new clothing for the sport - bloomers for
girls! They finally realized that skirts are impossible! I
hope this is the beginning of a fashion trend.*

*I must hurry now. See you at the pier! Love to all!
I can't wait to hug Ida and Frank!*

Love, love, love,

Gertrude

On Friday, Eleanor was surprised to discover
that Gertrude's next letter dated from January, 1892.
Eleanor knew, from the newspaper clipping, that by
that date Gertrude and Will were married. The return
address was a new one, too - Plymouth Meeting,
Pennsylvania. Eleanor read with interest:

Dear Lizzie,

*We are all settled at Tom and Helen
Hovenden's. We had a lovely New Year's. The
Hovendens had a party and many of their friends (and
Will's too, of course) came out from Philadelphia. It was
so nice to see faces from our Annisquam summers: Hugh
and Frank Jones, Stephen Parrish, Robert Vonnoh, and
Cecelia Beaux! And I finally met Alice Barber Stephens - -
she's the woman whose work I admired last year at the
Academy Show. Many of the artists who came are on the
hanging committee this year, and there is much talk about*

126

opening up the exhibition to show more of the New York and Boston artists, and to giving the impressionist pictures more of a prominent placement. It's going to be a wonderful exhibition, and I'm very much looking forward to the private opening!

I finally got to see the Mummer's Parade on New Year's Day! I didn't think anyone would want to wake up early enough to go after the party, but to my surprise they all declared themselves very happy to take me! It was clear, but freezing, so we bundled up tight and set off at 7 a.m. in order to get a good view. We hardly slept at all, but the early expedition turned out to be quite necessary. We found a good spot on Chestnut Street, almost in front, and the seemingly hundreds of people behind us could not possibly have seen anything, but there they stood, nevertheless! At least all those people kept us warm! The parade was so much fun, the local clubs were dressed in all sorts of costumes - cowboys and Indians, military men, devils and angels, historical and literary figures, everything you could think of! Apparently the competition between clubs is very fierce, for prizes are awarded for the best and most ingenious ideas, although no one could tell me exactly what the prizes were. Besides the costumed figures there were brass bands and drum corps, floats, horses, and the most delightful carriages. Frank and Ida would simply adore it - we must all come down together one year so they can see the parade.

Will is just finishing my second portrait. Thank goodness it is due at Avery Galleries later this month, for I don't think I can take much more of posing in the Hovenden's drafty studio! I don't know why I always think Pennsylvania is far enough south to make some difference in the winter weather - this year it seems to be even colder here than it is at home! We are going down with the paintings in a few weeks, and I think Mr. Avery will be very pleased with this year's results. Lizzie, I will tell you a secret - I don't want them to sell this portrait! I was devastated when "A Quiet Hour" sold. The portraits are so personal - all the props are from your home, and in this one I'm playing the piano I've played since I was a child, and most of all, Will has painted my engagement and wedding ring so prominently that I can't help but feel that this painting should belong only to me! Don't you agree, or am I being childish? Let me know your thoughts, for if you think I am right, I will ask Will not to let it be for sale.

There was an article in the paper about how to make bread, and Helen is letting me practice. I cannot seem to bake a loaf without it having a hole somewhere inside! Everyone has an opinion about this - I knead too much, or not enough, or I don't let the bread rest long enough before baking, or I let it rest too long! Help! The taste is good, but those darn holes! Let me know where you think I am going wrong.

Will and Tom have been playing checkers every evening and they get quite engrossed in the game! Helen and I are starting to tire of it, but it is so cold and dreary outside that it seems a shame to spoil their fun and insist that they stop and do something with us. We don't quite have the energy to bundle up and go out! I feel as if I am hibernating this winter, but it is a cozy feeling after all. Perhaps I will burst into spring with twice the energy I usually have after being so sedate for all these months!

I am starting to think about our trip to California. We still haven't decided on a departure date, but needless to say the "semi-tropical weather of sunny Santa Barbara" is a great magnet right now!

Perhaps we will surprise you all and hop on the train one day... I'll send you a postcard if we do!

Love to everyone... and most of all to you,

Gertrude

7

Saturday morning Miranda telephoned to invite
Eleanor and Peter to an afternoon barbecue.   Peter
was very excited to see Alan, for despite his casual
dismissal of spending his weekdays with him, Alan was
one of his favorite people, and he had deeply missed
seeing him the summer before. Alan Smith was two
years older than Peter, and the youngest child of
Miranda's youngest, Kelly. Kelly and Rob's two other
children were grown with young families of their own,
but Alan had been their "last folly," as Kelly loved to
say.   Apparently Kelly had reached her forties and
longed for another baby, so despite the inconvenience
of reliving the diaper stage, they had gone for it. Peter
thought Alan had it great - all the advantages of being
an only child, with the added advantage of having
doting older siblings, and parents who had experienced
it all before.

Eleanor, too, was looking forward to seeing
Kelly and Rob. She'd always had a fondness for Kelly,
because Bill had such happy memories of her as his
baby-sitter. When Kelly married Rob, Bill was still a
teenager, but in his twenties he gave them a unique
belated wedding present - he worked the memory of
their wedding into a story he was writing. Eleanor

always thought that was one of the most romantic gifts of which she had ever heard.

Eleanor and Peter arrived at the Cowling's at about two in the afternoon. The Cowling house was up on Squam Rock Road, near the gigantic boulder where a lovesick Indian maiden had purportedly jumped to her death. Peter had always been fascinated with the myth, and firmly believed that the rock was not high enough to kill anyone, but for obvious reasons was discouraged from testing this theory.

Kelly was the first one to spot them, and came running out of the house, shaking her large frame and throwing her arms wide open. "I'm so happy to see you!" she gushed. She gave them both a big bear hug and then sent Peter on to find Alan, tossing her arm around Eleanor's shoulder and escorting her into the house.

"Look who I found, Mother!" Kelly called out to Miranda, who was in the kitchen, turning over marinated chicken pieces in a large bowl. Rob was standing nearby, wearing a chef's apron and holding up a barbecue spatula.

"Just in time!" he called, waving a quick hello before turning to head for the patio. "I'm about to start the grill."

"I hope you're hungry," Kelly announced. "We've been cooking all day."

"Well, it won't be wasted on Peter," Eleanor said. "He's been an eating machine lately. Nathan says he has a hollow leg! He's been feeding him lunch every day because Peter is helping him with the houses this summer."

"Oh, how is Nathan?" Miranda asked. "Ellen Conboy is just delighted with the work he's doing.

You must see him often if Peter's working with him?"

Kelly grinned at Eleanor, then addressed her mother. "Mother, don't be subtle or anything! I'm sure Ellie knows all about you ladies' plans to marry her off again at the first chance you get! Don't mind them, Ellie, they're just old romantics."

Eleanor was blushing, and feeling very awkward. "It's all right. Nathan is a very nice person. I'm sure I would be honored to date him, if I was ready to date anyone."

Kelly was immediately apologetic. "Oh, Ellie, I didn't mean to imply that you should be dating already. Neither did mother. How awful of us! We were only teasing -- please don't take offense!"

"Kelly, you are such a trouble-maker," Miranda piped in. "I was really only asking an innocent question about Nathan! You think *I* don't know what Ellie's going through?"

"Sorry, Mom."

Miranda looked affectionately at Kelly. "Ever since you were a child you've known how to put a foot in my mouth!"

"Sorry, Mom," Kelly repeated, looking truly sheepish.

Eleanor felt obligated to speak up. "Really, it's okay! I'm not the least bit offended. I'm glad you all take an interest in me at all! Ever since I've come back to Annisquam, everyone's been so kind. I was afraid no one would want to have anything to do with me, without Bill. Now I see how silly that was."

"Oh, Ellie, how could you think that?" Miranda demanded. "You're as much as part of our family here as the rest of the Strayers. Why, we were very disappointed last summer when you and Peter didn't

132

come up. We all felt so keenly how little we'd been able to do for you, and then it seemed even worse when we realized we might never see you again. You know, you wouldn't be the first person to hide from the past when it could remind you of painful events. We were afraid you would abandon Annisquam forever."

"To be honest, I might have, if it wasn't for Peter. He wanted so badly to come back that I just couldn't sell the cottage. Anyway, I'm so glad now that I didn't. It would have been a terrible mistake. I've been happier since I've been back here than I've been in ages."

"Good for you!" Kelly enthused. "Sometimes it's best to face the past head-on. Sometimes it turns out to be just what you need."

"What turns out to be just what you need?" Rob asked. He had returned from lighting the grill.

"Oh, Ellie was just telling us that she hesitated to come back to Annisquam, since Bill died," Kelly explained to her husband.

Rob looked sympathetically at Eleanor. "That cottage must hold a lot of memories for you," he said.

"It does. More than you think," Eleanor added, thinking for a moment of the letters.

"You know, I remember the first time Bill ever told us about you, Ellie. Do you remember, Mother? We were right here in this kitchen. Bill came over to visit, and started gushing about some girl he'd been dating. How beautiful she was, what a great writer she was... It was the first time I ever heard him go on so about a girl. Your ears must have been burning that day, Ellie!"

"Really? Did Bill say I was a great writer?"

"Goodness, yes," Miranda concurred. "He thought you had the makings of the next Joyce Carol Oates. I'll never forget it! The first time I met you I thought you'd be so intellectual I'd be too embarrassed to speak!"

"Well, that certainly wasn't the case!" Eleanor exclaimed, but she was very surprised, and pleased. It meant a lot to her to believe that Bill really did think she had talent.

"Do you write now, Ellie?" Rob asked.

"No, I haven't written for years. Not really since I got married."

"Well, marriage will do that sometimes. But it's never too late! Isn't the world filled with great writers who started after they'd already had a long career at something else?" Kelly asked.

"Absolutely," Rob agreed with his wife. "I know lots of people who started new careers at mid-life, and are very successful. I would imagine that to be a great writer you have to live through some things yourself. I mean, I don't know if a person in their twenties really has the life experience it takes to write well."

"Wait a minute, Rob. Bill was a great writer, and he was young!" Kelly insisted, just before Eleanor had a chance to open her mouth and declare the same thing.

"Well, I always thought that Bill was old beyond his years. Very wise. Very unusual in a young person. Peter takes after him, though. I was just outside listening to the boys. Peter sounds like an adult sometimes. Have you noticed, Ellie?"

Eleanor agreed that Peter often surprised her with his maturity. "He really takes after his father,

134

doesn't he?"

"I remember when I used to baby-sit Bill," Kelly reminisced. "I always thought he ought to be the one baby-sitting. I used to get scared at any strange noises, and Bill was always having to reassure me! 'It's just the wind, Kelly,' he'd say, or 'That's the furnace, you silly goose!' I really don't know what the Strayers needed me for - - Bill could have gotten along just fine without me!"

Everyone laughed, and Eleanor felt comfortable again. It was nice to be around people who didn't hesitate to talk about Bill. Many of her friends back in Boston seemed to be afraid to mention him. But of course, they had lived through her most depressed period, when just his name would send her into deep melancholy, and make her unfit for any further conversation.

The chicken was sent to the grill, and dishes of salads - macaroni, potato and coleslaw - began to appear from the refrigerator. Fresh-baked rolls came out of the oven, baked beans came off of the stove, and a cherry pie was uncovered so that Eleanor would leave room for dessert. It was enough food to feed a small army, but the Cowlings, raised on Miranda's renowned cooking, were used to huge meals, and considered great amounts of leftovers to be the status-quo.

Everyone ate with gusto, and the mealtime conversation was filled with reminisces of Bill in his youth - which was of particular delight to Peter, who heard many of these stories for the first time. Midway through the meal, Peter mentioned that Eleanor had promised him Bill's old truck when he turned sixteen, but that he was unsure whether it would be wise to learn to drive on a stick shift, or on an automatic first.

He kindly neglected to mention that Eleanor could not drive the truck herself. Rob and Kelly disagreed on which transmission was better to start with - Kelly taking the position that it was infinitely easier to learn on an automatic. But Rob disagreed.

"It's not that difficult to learn how to drive a stick - in fact, it's easiest to learn it right from the beginning - and once you learn you never lose it. I've seen too many people put it off and then never do it. And that's a shame, because the true driving experience is that pure sensation of handling the car by hand - to feel the road and the car move in harmony, to have that control in difficult conditions or situations - that's real driving!"

"You make it sound Zen-like," Eleanor said with a touch of amusement.

"Sometimes when you're heading down a winding country road, all by yourself, shifting through the accelerations - it is Zen-like!" Rob exclaimed.

"Dad, tell Peter about shifting - the way you explained it to me. Tell him about thinking about the gears of a clock," Alan requested.

"Peter, what Alan's referring to is the way I learned myself. It's not technically accurate, but that's irrelevant - if you think of it this way your hands and feet will understand what to do. Imagine that the engine is filled with gears, each successive gear moving at an increased speed. The stick in your hand connects to another gear, call it the driving gear. You engage this driving gear with one of the other gears, like the wheels of a clock, when you want to move. So, in neutral the gears are not connected. You move the stick into first, and the car moves slowly, and can move up to a certain speed. To go faster you disengage from the first gear, and move into the second. That gear can move up to a faster speed. When you want to go even faster than second, you disengage and move into third. And so on. Do you get the picture?"

"Yes!" Peter had been listening with rapt attention.

"Dad let me try it in a parking lot a few weeks ago," Alan told everyone. "It worked great! I can't wait to drive."

"Well, your mother is not looking forward to it. Each child that's learned to drive has cost me five pounds and hundreds of grey hairs!" Kelly moaned. "I just rack myself with worry until they graduate from college!"

"Ah, Mom," Alan protested, "I'll be a good driver!"

"Your two siblings were good drivers too, but a mother worries, nevertheless."

Eleanor had been listening quietly to the conversation, considering Rob's explanation of driving a stick shift. It didn't sound nearly as difficult as she had always thought. She realized that she wished, very much, that she had learned to drive the truck. It would have been a nice gift to Bill. It would have meant a lot to him.

After supper Rob and the boys played catch in the backyard, and the women sipped iced tea in the family room. Miranda asked Eleanor if she had ever gone to the Historical Society, and Eleanor ended up explaining everything she knew about the Gertrude/Lizzie letters. Both Miranda and Kelly were impressed with the story, and interested in the fact that the Strayer cottage had been moved up from the point, but noted that it wasn't uncommon at all.

"You'd be surprised how many cottages have been moved in Annisquam," Miranda told her. "The town stretched up the hill as the years went by, and people seemed to do a lot more moving than building. I suppose if you liked your original home, it was cheaper to move it than to re-build it."

Miranda also had a few memories of the Langdon family, but not any that dated back close to the era of Gertrude. "You know, you probably should tell your story to Lydia," she encouraged Eleanor. "She's the one who spends the most time poking about in the Library and Historical Society. Maybe she knows something about all this. Anyway, she'd surely be interested."

Eleanor agreed that was a good idea. It was soon time to leave, and Peter and Eleanor said their good-byes, thanking the Cowlings for a wonderful afternoon. "It really was nice to hear all those stories of Bill," Eleanor gratefully acknowledged. "It did me a world of good. I've been dwelling on the bad times instead of the good times lately. You reminded me of why I loved him so much."

Miranda and Kelly looked at her with tears in their eyes. "Thank you, dear, for saying that," Miranda spoke first. "We do so want you to be happy here."

"Yes," Kelly agreed. "I miss him too. Let's get together again before I have to leave."

"We will," Eleanor promised. She and Peter waved good-bye and began walking back to their cottage.

* * * *

Later that evening, Eleanor unfolded the next letter. Gertrude was again on the move, this time writing from a train.

October 6, 1892

Dear Lizzie,

It was so much fun to receive your telegram at the Cheyenne depot! What a nice surprise! It's amazing, isn't it, that you can send a telegram from Boston and have it arrive in Cheyenne just when we do! Will and I were quite relieved, though, to find your message was just to say hello, and that no one back home was ill.

We are on the Southern Pacific line now, somewhere in Nevada. Although we are traveling in supreme comfort, the novelty of the experience is wearing off, and I am beginning to tire of the dust, and longing for a bed I do not need to fear falling out of! Perhaps I am also alarmed at the great distance we are traveling - it is so hard to comprehend how vast this nation is, until one has traveled it overland. It is majestic and beautiful, but the great space makes me feel that the loneliness must be terrible for the people who live in some of the very small towns we have passed through.

Will went back to the third class car the other day, just for amusement, but he came back not amused, but disturbed by the conditions. While we dine on roast beef and champagne and the finest delicacies, the emigrants have no water, no food except what they can grab at the depot stops, no linen, no real beds. He said it made him feel guilty that we should be so fortunate while others suffer so. He said there is even one mother with two small children, packed in there with all of the men, and that the smell is awful as it is impossible for anyone, or anything, to stay clean. I sent him back with some money for the mother, which he said she very gratefully received.

On a lighter note, tell Frank that we have encountered no train robbers and no Indians. However, there was a small herd of buffalo spotted in the distance in Wyoming. That was quite exciting! I was glad, however, that they were too far away for anyone to shoot.

We have also had excitement of another sort. There was a lady cardsharp on board for a while, and she managed to bilk some of the less-disciplined male passengers out of quite a bit of money! It was rather amusing to me, although not to the gamblers, who were perhaps more mortified at losing to a woman than depressed at simply losing. It serves them right for thinking she would be easily beaten!

Oh, I must tell you that our fellow passengers have by and large been delightful. There are a number of other people heading for Santa Barbara, so we will have some instant friends when we arrive. It has been torture for Will that the train never stops moving long enough for him to paint the scenery! I do believe he was tempted to jump off the train a few times, but luckily he has managed to control himself and be consoled with the wonders awaiting us in California.

Well, Lizzie, love to all. I will mail this at the next whistle stop, and the next time you hear from me I suspect I will be in Santa Barbara!

With all ~~my~~ _our_ love,

Gertrude _and Will_

Eleanor was amused to see that Will had marked out the word "my" and replaced it with "our," and then added his name to the closing. *I can just imagine him teasing her because she never mentions that he sends regards too!* she thought with a smile.

On Sunday Eleanor spent the day at Wingaersheek beach with Peter and Alan, sunning and reading while the boys splashed in the waves. The tide was so low that they were able to wade out about a half mile before there was any significant depth to the water. It was a perfect day and the beach was busy, but not so crowded that it felt claustrophobic. Eleanor told the boys that there used to be a ferry connecting the beach directly to Annisquam, and they were duly impressed, and wished it still existed so they could avoid the hot car ride home. That evening she and Peter rented a movie - an action film that Peter had been begging to see since he was about nine. It was obvious to Eleanor now that Peter was old enough for most R-rated movies, although she still felt it was her job to screen them first herself. They enjoyed the film, and were so tired by the time they headed up to bed, that Eleanor decided to skip her daily letter.

* * * *

The clouds rolled in the next day - along with the humidity - not bringing rain, but making the air feel sticky and thick. Eleanor took advantage of the overcast sky to do some gardening in the morning, but the heavy air caused her to soon be dripping with sweat. She took her second shower of the day, and wondered what to do with herself. There were groceries and cat food she needed, so she decided to drive up to the Star Market in Gloucester.

On the way to her car she was suddenly struck with an idea. What if she was to try to drive the truck? No one was around; she could succeed or fail in absolute privacy. Rob had made it sound so easy the other day - surely she could do it with enough determination. Almost before she had convinced herself it was worth the effort, her arms were lifting up the garage door and her fingers were groping for the keys on the hook inside the tool cabinet. She slid onto the red vinyl seat and looked at the dashboard and stickshift. Then she tested the feel of the clutch. *Okay,* she thought to herself, *here it goes.*

The key turned easily in the ignition, and she sat there for a moment, foot on the brake and the truck in neutral, before taking a deep breath and pressing the clutch. She moved the stick into reverse, and slowly let the clutch up. The truck stalled.

"Darn!" she exclaimed out loud, but she knew what was wrong. She hadn't moved her foot to the accelerator. *When you step off the brake,* she instructed herself, *give the car some gas.* She tried it again, and found herself moving slowly out of the garage and down the driveway towards the street.

"Oh my God!" she said, somewhat panicked and somewhat thrilled. "Okay, stop after you swing onto the street!" She was talking to herself, which was almost as comforting as having someone else to talk to. "Okay, there. Now carefully put the gear in first."

This took a couple of tries. Planter's Neck was on a hill, and every time she took her foot off the brake she began to roll backward before she could get the truck into gear. Finally she got up the nerve to do it quickly enough that she didn't roll. The next thing she knew she was moving forward.

First gear was easy, and Eleanor wished briefly that she could drive in first all the way to Gloucester. However, the fastest way there involved getting on the highway, and Eleanor knew that 10 miles per hour wouldn't cut it after she left town. *You can do this, you can do this*, she repeated over and over again to herself. *Think of the gears of a clock.*

During every second of the twenty minute drive to the market Eleanor's nerves were on edge, and she was hyper-conscious of every yield, stop, or turn that could cause her to stall. Miraculously, although she stalled a few times in Riverdale, she managed to get on the highway smoothly, and only stalled one more time, just as she pulled into her spot in the supermarket parking lot. She pulled up the parking brake and bounced out of the truck. *I did it!* she thought to herself, throwing her arms over her head in a victory grip. *Yes!*

She was dripping with sweat and laughingly realized she'd need yet another shower when she got back home, but her happiness was unbounded. She practically sang her way through the grocery store, and only suffered a split second of hesitation when she contemplated the drive back again to Annisquam. But she pooh-poohed it right out of her mind. *You can do it*, she assured herself. *You definitely can.*

The drive home was easier, and she only stalled once. By the time she pulled into the driveway, she was feeling as if she could conquer the world. Then to her surprise, as she re-hung the keys in the cabinet, she looked back at the truck and felt tears form in her eyes.

She knew exactly why she was crying.

"Bill," she whispered out loud. "I wish you could see this. Can you see it? Are you somewhere up there, proud of me? Oh Bill, I am so sorry I never did this while you were alive. Please, if you are out there, know that I love you with all my heart." Tears rolled down her face, but they were tears of both joy and sorrow, and they felt as good as they felt bad. *I did this for you*, she thought to herself. Then she added, *And for me too.*

Later, when Peter came home, Eleanor suggested that they go out and return the movie, and pick up some Chinese food. She had a twinkle in her eye that Peter didn't pick up. "Sure!" he agreed eagerly and headed out the front door towards the car, parked on the street. Eleanor followed and turned towards the driveway. "Where are you going?" she asked him innocently.

"I thought you said we were driving into Gloucester," he said, looking at her with confusion.

"We are, but we're taking the truck."

"What?!"

"Come on, I'll show you."

Peter followed his mother with a bemused expression on his face, which quickly turned to amazement as she bid him to get in the truck, and effortlessly drove the vehicle out of the garage. Peter was bouncing up and down with pleasure and excitement. "Boy, Mom this is great! I can't believe you taught yourself! Wait till I tell everybody!"

"Now, I'm not that good yet, so don't be surprised if we stall a couple of times," Eleanor warned him, but to both their delight she managed to get to the video store without one single stall, and only stalled once between the Chinese restaurant and home.

On the way into the house, Peter suddenly threw his arm around his mother and kissed her on the cheek. "I'm so proud of you, Mom," he said, and Eleanor glowed for the rest of the evening.

* * * *

Before opening the next letter, Eleanor thought to herself that for once she had done something that was like Gertrude - brave and spontaneous. She began to read in anticipation of Gertrude's latest adventure. The letterhead was engraved *Lincoln House, Santa Barbara, California.*

November 8, 1892

Dear Lizzie,

You will not believe where I am actually situated as I write this letter. I am sitting along the bank of a dirt road, at the edge of a broad plain, looking straight up into the Sierra Madre mountains. Along the road in front of me is a mudwagon, with a driver and four horses, and beside me Will is painting. Yes, you guessed it - the driver is modeling and the wagon is hired for the day! We rode out in it from Santa Ynez, after taking the stagecoach to that point. It cost us fifty dollars to rent the wagon, horses and driver for the half-day! The owner of the stable thought we were only a little strange when he found out what we wanted it for. The driver, however, was extremely flattered, and said he was "down-right pleased to pose for our picture!" I believe he can't wait to get home to tell his wife!

The stagecoach ride to Santa Ynez was so funny! The coach was filled with very proper East Coast tourists, but nevertheless the driver read the rules to us, which were posted on the ceiling and consisted of things such as: No liquor, unless you share with the driver; tobacco chewing is allowed but you must spit with the wind, not against it; no rough language, except for the driver; topics of discussion must not include religion, politics or stagecoach accidents; and don't use your neighbor's shoulder for a pillow! Everything out here is so colorful, and larger than life. Even the locals seem to be placed here for our entertainment, or perhaps the contrast between we New Englanders and our western American and Spanish counterparts is just so great that it lends itself to a sense of constant absurdity!

But it is also all so delightful! Everyone is friendly, especially at our boarding house. The Lincoln is charming, and just as we'd heard it is built New England style, which adds to our sense of displacement. It has a widow's walk, and the Chinese cook climbs up there everyday, and looks through a spyglass to see how many new guests are arriving by train or ship. By the time they arrive he has dinner waiting for them! Our room is kept stocked with all the oranges, figs, almonds and pomegranates we can eat, and the whole building is filled with vases of fresh flowers, which they pick from their own gardens.

The dining room has quite a reputation, and the other day a most amazing coincidence occurred. We were seated at a table with a lovely couple, and naturally we made introductions, and they announced that they were Cyrus and Elizabeth Upham. Will immediately informed

146

them that his mother was an Upham, and sure enough, this gentleman is also descended from the original John Upham who landed in Massachusetts in 1635! Will and he know very few people in common, as the family is so large, and Cyrus' part is originally from Iowa. Still, it was amazing - here we are, at the other end of the country, and still meeting relatives!

Cyrus and his wife are visiting from Pasadena, but are quite impressed with Santa Barbara, and are thinking of opening a hotel here. We told them we'd be delighted to let the family back East know. Family alone could probably keep the hotel full for hundreds of years!

Mr. Lincoln, the former owner of the hotel but now head of the First National Gold Bank, has offered to take Will and me to the Montecito Hot Springs Hotel for a mineral bath. Apparently this is a treat not to be missed, since the hotel is actually a private club, and very exclusive. Mr. Lincoln is an art lover, and had heard something of Will's work, and came over to make our acquaintance last week. He has also promised to introduce us to Alexander Harmer, a local artist who is quite well thought of. I am actually more interested in meeting Mr. Harmer's fiancé, Senorita Felicidad Abadie, who is the daughter of an old Spanish family, and reputed to be one of the most beautiful women in California.

I have been sitting here for two hours and have only written those six paragraphs. I keep getting distracted by the scenery. It is absolutely silent here, except for the occasional restless movements of the horses, and the calling of birds. An eagle flew overhead just a few minutes ago, and a fox crossed the road behind us earlier, but luckily the horses didn't notice it. The ground is covered with rough grasses and plants - nothing like our smooth Eastern grasses - and I keep having to shift position to keep the *briars from getting bothersome. Still, there is something so peaceful and majestic about this place. I keep hearing words from Reverend Young's sermons as I look around, as if the landscape had moral lessons to teach me.*

Will has gotten permission to paint the gardens of the Mission, and I know they will be lovely and peaceful too, but I prefer my religion with a touch of wildness. I like to feel that God is overwhelming me with nature.

Mama must be home from Annisquam by now, so give her my love. And of course love to William and Ida and Frank. I am going to try to write to Nellie and Minnie before we have to leave today. I brought a large supply of writing paper, and I'm glad that I don't sew or I would probably be knitting or embroidering instead of writing during these painting expeditions!

Love always,

Gertrude

The next day, Eleanor's phone rang at noon.

"Peter's been talking all morning about how you taught yourself to drive the pickup." It was Nathan. "I had to call and congratulate you."

"Thanks. I'm pretty proud of myself, I must admit."

"So when are we going to dinner?"

Eleanor was caught off guard, and tried to postpone the inevitable, but only succeeded in stumbling over her answer: "I don't know. Geez, Nathan. Not now. In a few weeks, maybe?"

"How about this Saturday? You can drive."

Eleanor laughed despite her discomfort. "You may not want to eat after you get through riding with me. Your stomach may be in knots."

"I'll take my chances. Say, seven o'clock?"

"I don't know, Nathan."

"It's only a meal, remember? You need to get out more."

She gave in. "Well, all right. But only a meal, like you said."

"Just a meal between friends," Nathan concurred.

Eleanor hung up the phone and sat down at the kitchen table. She had butterflies in her stomach already. She felt sick, but also excited. *This must be what it feels like to have an affair*, she thought. *I feel like I'm cheating on Bill.* In the next instant she was able to convince herself that she was being absurd. *Even if it is a date*, she reasoned, *I have been a widow for two years. It can't be a crime to go out to dinner with someone.* She promised herself she would put it out of her mind until she absolutely had to think of it, until Saturday if possible.

In the meantime, some practice driving the truck was probably a good idea. Eleanor decided to track down Gabby and surprise her. She found the Newsome phone number easily in the phone book. "Gabby? Hi, it's Eleanor Strayer. I'm learning to drive the pickup truck. Want to come for a ride?"

Gabby was obviously amused. "So, you want an eye witness in case of accidents I suppose." She let out a mock sigh. "I guess that's what friends are for."

"Great! I'll pick you up in a few minutes."

"Give me ten. I'm just swallowing my lunch."

"Okay. Bye." Eleanor hung up the phone, elated. Suddenly she felt as if all was right with the world. For the first time in years, she was living. She was on her own and she was living. *Like a normal person. With something to live for.*

Gabby was waiting outside for her when she pulled up to the Newsome home, and they sat in the truck for a moment, deciding where to go. "Let's go to Essex," Gabby suggested. "We can look in the antique shops. Plus, it isn't too dangerous a drive. Sort-of straight roads, if you know what I mean."

Eleanor assured her that she really wasn't that bad a driver, and in fact, made it to Essex without a single stall. Gabby was impressed, and announced that she'd trust her to drive anywhere. They parked on the side of the Main Street, down at the end where the shops first started. "We can walk up one side and down the other," Gabby said, with her usual energy.

Gabby collected antique pens, and was eager to see what new ones the shops might have. Eleanor decided to look at paintings, with the almost impossible hope that she might find an undiscovered Picknell. The first few shops were full of good antiques but horrid paintings - old, but amateur works. At the fourth shop the general quality of paintings looked much better, and she asked the owner if he had ever heard of Picknell. He assured her that yes, he had once handled a fine one, but sold it almost immediately to an art dealer in Boston. "Fine paintings like that don't last long down here," he told her. "Every Boston dealer has their spies keeping an eye out for the good stuff."

Sure enough, in the other shops with fine paintings, there were no Picknells, and the dealers concurred that his works would be unlikely finds. However, one dealer told her that he had a friend who owned one and lived in the area, and that he would give her name and number to this person. If this friend was willing to let her see it he would be in touch.

By the time they climbed back into the truck the day was waning and Gabby had added two pens to her collection, although she protested to Eleanor that she should never have come out with her because she could ill afford her new purchases. Despite that Eleanor knew she had enjoyed herself tremendously. She dropped the younger woman off at home, and pulled up into her own driveway. Peter and Nathan were sitting on the porch steps, drinking lemonade and waiting for her.

"Hey Mom, where've you been? Nathan came by to see you."

"So I see. How long have you two been waiting?"

"Not long," Nathan replied. "Have you been out doing research?"

"In a way. Gabby Newsome and I went to Essex, and I looked in the antique stores on the off chance that there might be some Picknell paintings hanging around in some dusty corner. But of course there weren't."

Peter got up and stretched. "I'm going in to shower. Alan invited me over tonight."

"Do you want dinner?" his mother asked.

"Before I go to the Cowling house, with all that food? Are you kidding?" Peter laughed and disappeared into the house. Eleanor sat down next to Nathan.

"Nice driving there, Ellie. You look good behind the wheel of the truck."

"Very funny, Nathan. All you saw me do was turn into the driveway."

"Yes, and you did it without running over anything, so I'd say it was pretty fine driving."

Eleanor smiled at him. "You're silly."

"I hope so. I don't think I could win you over if I was too serious."

Eleanor became silent, and Nathan was conscious of having said too much. The words "win you over" hung in the air between them, and neither one of them knew how to get beyond the words without difficulty. Finally Eleanor, with a weak smile, changed the subject.

"One of the dealers said he had a friend with a Picknell painting. He's going to give the friend my phone number. I'd love to see more of his works."

"Have you called or written the Museum of Fine Arts? They probably have a lot of information on Picknell."

"No, I hadn't thought of that. Thanks, that's a great idea! In Gertrude's latest letter she writes about being with Will while he's painting, in California. I would love to see that painting."

"Well, the museum may know which other museums have his works. You should be able to get reproductions of the ones in public collections."

"Yes, I'll do that." They sat there quietly for a few moments. Eleanor heard the sounds of children coming up from the beach, and the bustle of her neighbors' slamming doors and scraping lawn chairs. "It's getting to be the busy season, isn't it?" she asked absently.

"Listen, Ellie," Nathan suddenly spoke, "I'm sorry about before. I mean, I don't want to put any pressure on you. I really enjoy your company, Ellie, and I don't want there to be any awkwardness between us. If I ever get on your nerves, I want you to tell me, okay? Promise you'll let me know!"

Eleanor looked seriously at him. "I will let you know," she promised, "but why do you want to spend time with me anyway? I'm a mess, trust me! I'm just not ready for this."

Nathan reached over, gently placed his hand under her chin, and looked her straight in the eyes. "I want to be with you because you are the most kind, generous and beautiful woman I have ever known, and because I see now that you are just on the verge of becoming someone truly extraordinary, and I want to be there when it happens." This speech was so remarkable that Eleanor simply blushed and stared at him. The moment was interrupted by Peter coming out of the house behind them.

"Well, I'm out of here," he announced.

"I'll walk with you," Nathan said quickly, standing up. "I'll see you Saturday, okay, Ellie?"

"Okay."

"And I'll drive if you want," he added with a smile.

Eleanor laughed. "Perhaps that's a good idea after all," she said, realizing that she was going to be incredibly nervous on Saturday.

Eleanor wandered into her house in a daze. Nathan's words were ringing in her ears. "You are on the verge of becoming someone truly extraordinary." What did he mean? Was it true? And, most confusing of all, why should it be happening now; why couldn't it have been the case when she was with Bill?

She made herself some soup, although it was far too warm for hot liquids. *Comfort food*, she thought to herself. *Chicken soup for the soul*. She sat with a mug on the back porch and tried to make sense of her relationship with Nathan. *Why is it not just a plain, platonic friendship?* she asked herself. *I don't understand why there is something more going on here.* It remained incomprehensible to Eleanor - she didn't want a relationship, and yet it seemed to be happening. She tried to concentrate on how much she missed Bill, and refused to examine her feelings for Nathan, because she knew, deep down, that she would find she liked him, and she enjoyed his company. And Eleanor still believed that love was eternal and immutable, and that to feel it for anyone else would belie her relationship with Bill.

Shivering, despite the heat, she wandered upstairs and almost without thinking reached for the packet of letters. The return address suddenly startled her from her reverie, and instantly she forgot all about her own concerns.

December 15, 1892
The Cottage Hospital
Santa Barbara, California

Dear Lizzie,

There is no change. I have been by Will's bed for a week, and they have done all sorts of tests, but they still don't know what is wrong. His breathing is still labored, but mostly we are able to keep him comfortable. He eats a little now and then, but not enough to keep up his strength. I am so afraid, Lizzie! I realize now how much I miss you all, and how awful it is to be so far from home. Everyone is very kind to me, but I am so alone! How I wish I could press a magic button, and have you all appear by my side!

I wonder if it was the springs, after all, that made him sick. Everyone out here says that is impossible - the springs are used to cure ills, not cause them. But it is so odd, Lizzie, he was fine one day and then so suddenly ill the next!

I will write again when there is any change.

Love,
Gertrude

Eleanor held her breath and reached for the next letter. It was impossible that Will was going to die now, wasn't it? According to the Boston Museum book, he didn't die until 1897. Her hands were shaking as she unfolded the next letter.

January 1, 1893

The Cottage Hospital
Santa Barbara, California

Dear Lizzie,

Will is resting much easier and I have some wonderful news for the New Year - the doctors expect us to be able to check out this week, and Will can complete his convalescence at the hotel. He is gaining color and strength every day! He even asked for a sketch pad yesterday, so he could do a little drawing. I think he needed to feel that his hands would still work, and the lines he made were strong and sure. He is going to be fine, Lizzie! I thank God every minute that we have survived this.

I hope my telegram arrived in time for Christmas, because it was the only present I was able to send this year. But I knew it was the only present you wanted. What an odd Christmas we spent in the hospital, yet the staff did everything to make it jolly. And it was, of course, with the good news of his beginning recovery. The nurses and staff made the hospital look festive - they decorated all the rooms, and the hallways, and served turkey for dinner. They even brought Will a present - a small cactus in a pot with a Christmas ribbon around it. Only the smell of antiseptic kept us aware of our unusual location.

I am so tired, Lizzie. I think I will sleep for ten days straight when we get back to the hotel. Oh Lizzie, thank you for your prayers, and everyone else's! Tell them how much I love them and appreciate it! I must send a quick note now to Will's family, as they have also been worried sick about him. I will write again soon, or telegraph.

Much love,

Gertrude

Eleanor sighed with relief. Then in an instant she recognized the inevitable fact that Will was going to die only a few years later, and that she would have no choice but to read about it. *I must be prepared*, she reminded herself. *These letters won't always be happy.*

It also occurred to Eleanor that Gertrude was not going to take it well. Eleanor remembered only too well the first line of the last letter: "Ever since Will died, my life has been meaningless." That letter was written in 1903, six years after Will's death. For the first time, Eleanor had doubts about finishing the letters. *I don't want to relive the misery*, she thought. *I'm just now starting to get over it.*

But there was a strange pull to the whole thing - a strange attraction. What were Gertrude's thoughts those six years; why did she remain in a state of depression for so long? And, Eleanor couldn't help wondering, was there something she ought to learn from that, something perhaps, that would show her that her current good feelings were an illusion, or, even more importantly, that feeling better was wrong in some great moral sense?

Whatever lesson Gertrude had to teach, it was impossible now for Eleanor to pull away. She thought of Gertrude as her soul mate, and she would share whatever fate had in store for her.

Eleanor awoke the next morning with a new idea - why not drive back to Boston and visit the Art Museum in person? She had the whole day ahead of her and nothing specific planned. She showered and dressed, and realizing that Peter was already at work, left him a note saying she had gone back to town and might be home late.

Just as she was heading out the door the phone rang. An elderly male voice was on the other end. "Mrs. Strayer?" he asked tentatively.

"Yes?" Eleanor replied.

"I'm Samuel Hopstedder. My friend, Jeremy O'Connor, mentioned that you were interested in the artist William Lamb Picknell."

"Oh, yes! The antique dealer... he said he would give you my number."

"Yes. I have a very fine painting by the artist. Mr. O'Connor thought you would like to see it."

"Very much! It would mean a lot to me. I'm doing some research on the artist's wife, but I haven't actually seen very many of Picknell's paintings."

"I understand you're living in Annisquam? I'm in Gloucester. Would you like to come out today?"

"Oh, I was just heading out for the day. Would

tomorrow be all right?"

"Yes, say, after lunch? About 2:00?"

Eleanor told him that would be wonderful, and wrote down the directions he gave her. Before Mr. Hopstedder signed off, he mentioned that he looked forward to meeting her, and hearing about her own work.

My own work? Eleanor hoped she wouldn't disappoint him. She wondered, for a moment, what explanation she would give for her extensive interest in Gertrude's life, but decided she'd simply see how the meeting went and figure out then how much to tell him.

Eleanor drove to Boston, and the woman at the information desk of the Museum of Fine Arts directed Eleanor to the library. There she was asked to sign in, and state which institution she was from. Eleanor looked up helplessly at the nearest library assistant. "I'm afraid I'm not with an institution. I'm just curious."

"Oh, that's okay," he said reassuringly. "It's a slow day. What can I do for you?"

"I'd like some information on William Lamb Picknell. The Museum owns a painting of his."

"Actually, we own two, although they are not both hanging. What exactly do you want to know?"

"Well, I came by today to see if you had any illustrations of other paintings by him. Or if you had information on where other paintings might be. I mean, other museum collections."

"Let me get the file out. Have a seat at that table and I'll bring over whatever is pertinent," he added, motioning to an inner part of the library.

Eleanor sat down and a few minutes later the

160

assistant was standing before her with a manila file. "I xeroxed two items for you. Look that over and come get me if you want to know anything else."

Eleanor opened the file, and the first thing that caught her eye was a list of paintings from an exhibition. A cover sheet indicated it was Picknell's memorial exhibition, held at the Museum of Fine Arts from February to March of 1898. There were forty-four paintings listed. Most of the paintings had titles that were only descriptive - such as "Nearing Sunset" and "Early Morning" - and did not indicate where they might have been painted. But Eleanor was pleased to see that number thirty-two was titled "Mission Garden - Santa Barbara." Gertrude had mentioned that Will was planning to paint the garden, and apparently the painting had been a success - for this work was loaned by a collector, as were perhaps a dozen other works in the exhibition. Of these collectors, one was listed as Miss Ellen M. Picknell, and Eleanor wondered if this was the artist's sister, Nellie.

Eleanor was disappointed that there were no illustrations, for pictures were what she had really come to see. However, the next item in the file was a catalogue from the Executor's Sale, held in New York in January of 1900. Inside was a list of seventy-one paintings, but best of all, ten of these were illustrated. Someone, the same person who had recorded the prices each painting achieved, had written the titles of these ten works underneath each illustration, so that Eleanor was delighted to see before her a crisp and clear image of a painting titled "In California," which she recognized immediately as the one of the wagon and cart by the mountains discussed in Gertrude's letter. The painting was listed in the catalogue as 66 x 49 inches, which Eleanor noted must be width by height. *My goodness!* Eleanor thought, *How did they ever manage traveling around with canvases that size?*

In addition, the Executor's Sale had a cover page which included a list of nine public institutions which owned works by the artist. These included the Metropolitan Museum of Art, the Pennsylvania Academy of Fine Arts, and the Corcoran Art Gallery in Washington, D.C. *I can contact all these places and get reproductions of the paintings*, Eleanor recalled from her conversation with Nathan.

Eleanor got up to thank the library assistant, and asked him about the other Picknell owned by the Museum, other than "Morning on the Loing."

"It's called 'Sand Dunes of Essex,'" he told her, "but it's in storage. Wait a second and I'll show you an image." He stepped back into an inner room, and returned a few minutes later holding a photograph. "Here it is," he said, handing her the photo.

Eleanor found herself looking at a black & white image of a huge sand dune, with a field of sand and grass along side it. A sand road split the picture, and along the road in the distance was a cart and horse. "He seems to like to put carts and horses in his paintings," she noted.

The assistant agreed. "Do you know the painting in the Corcoran, 'The Road to Concarneau?'" he asked. "That's his most famous painting. It's a white road in France with a horse and cart going along it. You should see it some time, it won an honorable mention at the Paris Salon of 1880."

"Really?"

"Oh, yes. It was a big deal - the first time an American artist won honorable mention for a landscape. That painting made his reputation. One critic called it 'the greatest painting of sunshine ever painted.'"

"I think I do remember something about that," Eleanor said, recalling that Gertrude had mentioned it in her first letter. "You seem to know a lot about him," she added.

"Well, I like his work. You know, our "Morning on the Loing" was the painting that finally won him a full medal at the Salon, in 1895."

Two years before he died, Eleanor noted to herself. "Can I call you sometime if I go home and find out I have a lot more questions?" she inquired.

"Sure, here's my card. Call me anytime; I'm usually here at the desk."

Eleanor thanked the library assistant again, and wandered through the museum until she was standing in front of "Morning on the Loing." The painting depicted an impossibly perfect sunny day, and two large barges moored in a river of reflecting clear water. There was something about the brilliant sky, green grass and crystal water full of the sky's blue reflection that was almost too bright to look at. Eleanor always felt in looking at the painting that she ought to shade her eyes. "That's what makes it so amazing," she said out loud. "It's so real."

To Eleanor's surprise, someone answered her. "They call that technique the 'glare aesthetic.' Picknell was the best there was at it; most of the other practitioners were Europeans."

Eleanor turned around to find herself face-to-face with a small man wearing a brown suit and sporting small-framed glasses. Behind the glasses were piercing dark eyes, but the mop of hair on top of his head was blond. He was impossible to place in age, but he looked very much like a museum scholar. "I'm sorry, I didn't realize anyone was listening" she said, as way of introduction. "Are you the curator?" she asked timidly.

"Visiting," he replied. "My name is Brian Suskind," he added, "I'm here from Harvard. And you are...?"

"Eleanor Strayer."

"Very nice to meet you, Eleanor." He held out his hand. "It's nice to meet a Picknell fan. Are you by any chance related to Bill Strayer, the writer?"

"Yes, he was my husband."

"Fine man. I knew him briefly at Harvard. Wonderful writer. I've read all his books."

Eleanor could tell that Brian Suskind was not the kind to exaggerate, so she was impressed. "What brings you to the museum today?" she asked.

"I'm on sabbatical from sabbatical. I've been in France this past year studying the artists who worked in Pont Aven, one of whom was our Mr. Picknell. I'm home for a few weeks to see family."

"I don't know much about Picknell's work in France. When was he in Pont Aven?"

"Middle of the 1870s to the early 1880s. Made his reputation before he came home, as I'm sure you know."

Eleanor didn't want to admit she had only just heard the full story of that success not five minutes previously, so she just nodded her head.

"I wrote an article this spring about the Pont Aven colony," Mr. Suskind continued. "It was published in *American Art Review*. Did you see it?" Eleanor shook her head. "I can give you the reference if you are interested," he added.

Eleanor assured him that she was, and he pulled a business card out of a fancy gold case, and wrote the article reference on the reverse. "You can get the magazine in any good library," he told her.

Eleanor thanked him for the information and then found herself saying, "My interest is also in Picknell's wife, Gertrude. I'm doing research on her life."

"Really?" Brian Suskind was quite intrigued. "However did you get interested in her?"

"I found some letters she had written to her sister."

"You do plan on publishing your findings, don't you?" the small man asked, as if that was the only possible reason for doing research.

Eleanor was taken aback. "I hadn't thought about it," she admitted. "I was only curious."

"One can't keep these things to oneself," he insisted. "Scholarship must be shared! Surely your husband would have wanted you to publish your findings."

Eleanor didn't like the patronizing tone of this last statement, but she found herself too curious to end the conversation. "How would I publish my findings, if I wanted to?" she asked.

"Call me when you've written something up. I've got lots of connections. I'll put you in touch with the right editor."

Eleanor found herself thanking Mr. Suskind again, and then she turned to walk away. "Don't forget to call me!" the scholar called after her. "The world awaits your discovery!" Eleanor thought that was rather funny, but suppressed a giggle because she didn't want to appear rude.

Eleanor drove straight to the public library after leaving the museum, and easily found the article Brian Suskind had written. She found it was far more interesting than she had expected, for the art colony in Pont Aven had been active and important for many years, launching many a well-known art career. Not only was Picknell's early career described, but a number of the other artists mentioned in Gertrude's letters - the Jones brothers, Thomas Hovenden, and his future wife, Helen Corson - were also discussed. With satisfaction Eleanor noticed that the article emphasized the esteem with which Picknell was regarded by his fellow artists, and how he became the unofficial leader of the art colony after the death of Robert Wylie, an older artist and Picknell's mentor. Eleanor made a copy of the article so she could read it again later.

By the time she left the library, Eleanor realized she was famished. On a whim she telephoned a Boston friend, Hillary White, to see if she would meet her for coffee at Starbucks. To her delight Hillary was free, and they spent a lovely afternoon sipping coffee and dipping biscotti, and filling each other in on their separate summers. At the end of the afternoon, Hillary commented that she hadn't seen Eleanor looking and feeling so good in ages, and that the summer air of Annisquam must be better suited to her temperament than the crowded summer streets of Boston. Eleanor assured her that she was doing much better, and the two women parted feeling that their friendship had just been given a much-needed rejuvenation.

That night Gertrude's letter showed another change of locale.

May 3, 1893
The Palmer House
Chicago, Illinois

Dear Lizzie,

We have arrived at last in Chicago. But all is confusion in the Fine Arts building! The American Arts section officially opened two days ago with the rest of the Fair, but then Mr. Kurtz tried to close the galleries for a few days in order to finish hanging, as all the pictures have not yet been placed. This caused such an outrage that the poor man has been forced to re-open while he tries to find space for all the paintings, which number in the thousands it seems to me. I don't envy his job and yet I cannot excuse his not having managed to finish it on time; it really is unfair to the artists.

Luckily, Will's four paintings were sent early and they were well hung. I don't know that they will get much attention, however. As I said there seem to be thousands of paintings. If I, who have so much interest, find my head spinning after just seeing a few galleries, how much sooner will the uneducated art lover give up on trying to make any sense of it all? The paintings are not hung with any plan that I can see. Landscapes and figure pieces and portraits and historical subjects are all hung together, up and down the wall, no matter what their style. Will is not put off by this as I am - he says the individual merit of each work should speak for itself - but I think it is too tiresome to try to see the individual merit of works when they are all jumbled together in hot, crowded galleries!

As for the rest of the Fair, it is delightful! Imagine grand white buildings as if from an ancient arcadia, floating on a blue Venetian lake, and you will have a good idea of how beautiful it is. I must admit it gives you a thrilling sense of progress and pride to see the great statue of Republic overseeing it all. And at night, when it is all lit up from electric lights! You feel as if you can see the future, stretching out before mankind like the Milky Way!

After spending so many hours in the Fine Arts building, we were too tired to go inside any other buildings today, but we plan to explore the rest of the Fair before we leave. I, of course, want to go to the Midway and ride the Ferris wheel, but I will have to use all my charms to get Will to agree to it!

We will be home in just over a week. Love to everyone - it will be so good to see you all after so much time! I hope I will recognize Ida and Frank - they must have grown so much!

Love and kisses,

Gertrude

Eleanor was at first confused about the meaning of "the Fair;" then she remembered that 1893 was the year of the World's Columbian Exposition in Chicago. She had read about it in a cultural history course in college, but she would never have known that Picknell had participated. *There is a lot of valuable historical information in these letters,* she noted to herself. *Perhaps it wouldn't be that absurd after all to publish something about them.* She decided to give some consideration to Brian Suskind's suggestion, but in the meantime, she was determined to find some descendants before publishing, *in case they want to keep the letters private,* she thought.

* * * *

At two the next afternoon, Eleanor found herself knocking on the door of a contemporary townhouse nestled above Good Harbor Beach in Gloucester. Eleanor had expected Mr. Hopstedder to live in an older home, simply because he was an elderly man who collected antique paintings, but she soon realized how naive that expectation had been. As soon as Samuel Hopstedder opened the door, Eleanor's eye was drawn to the back wall of the living room, where a large beach scene by Picknell was hanging. Except for the painting, the room was completely contemporary - but the landscape suited it perfectly. The clean, sharp lines of the furniture were reflected in the crisp portrayal of the sand, sea and sky. Fluffy white clouds floating above a breeze-swept beach were mirrored in the actual sky seen through a window to the left of the painting.

"Oh...," Eleanor entered, already exclaiming over the painting, "It's beautiful!"

"You recognize it immediately, huh?" Mr. Hopstedder was a kindly looking man with a thick white mustache and thinner white hair. "My wife and I bought that painting way back in the seventies, when nobody had ever heard of Picknell. Got it cheap, too. But we always loved it! Now dealers call me up periodically trying to convince me to sell, but I never will, not while there's breath still left in this body. I promised Heddy that, and I intend to keep that promise."

"Heddy was your wife?" Eleanor asked politely.

Mr. Hopstedder nodded. "Fifty-two years. Wonderful woman. Best wife in the world."

Mr. Hopstedder's eyes had filled with tears, and in fear that hers would also, Eleanor hurriedly changed the subject. "It looks like it was painted in Annisquam. Does it say where it was done?"

"No. There's nothing on the back. I know it had to have been painted somewhere around here, though. I don't believe he painted anywhere else in Massachusetts."

There was a pause in the conversation while they both stood and admired the painting. Finally Mr. Hopstedder spoke, "Can I get you some coffee? Tea? Soda?"

"Coffee would be lovely, if it isn't too much trouble."

"No trouble at all. I'll be back in a jiffy."

The older man disappeared into the kitchen, and Eleanor sat down in a chair across from the painting, and continued to examine it. There were stray bits of sandgrass poking up in the foreground; it looked as if one could touch them. Eleanor walked over to the painting and very gently touched the surface. The paint was textured. Mr. Hopstedder walked in and handed her a mug.

"He used a palette-knife to get that effect - built up the surface so it gives you the feel of real beach. I paint some myself, so I can tell how he did it."

"Did he use a palette-knife in the sky too?" Eleanor asked him, as she noticed the way the clouds seemed to push the sky towards the viewer.

"All over. The man was a genius with the knife. They say he could paint so quickly that the eye could hardly follow it. Only worked in oils, however. At least that's all I've ever seen by him."

Eleanor dragged her eyes away from the

170

painting. "Are any of your paintings here too?" she asked, with real interest.

"That's one over there." Mr. Hopstedder pointed to an abstract work in blue and yellow on the wall behind her. "Not quite like a Picknell, huh?" he added, laughing.

Eleanor smiled. "It looks great in the room with it, though," she told him.

"So, young lady, sit down and tell me about your interest in Picknell. What brings you out here?"

Eleanor and Samuel sat down around the coffee table, and the older gentleman offered her a piece of shortbread from a plate he had brought from the kitchen. Eleanor took one and slowly munched, saying between bites, "Well, as I mentioned on the phone, my real interest is in Picknell's wife. I found a bunch of letters she wrote to her sister. They were in our attic, and I've been trying to figure out how they came to be there."

"You live in Annisquam, right?"

"Yes. The house has been in the family since 1905. But Picknell died in 1897, and there doesn't seem to be a connection between his family and ours."

"Interesting! Do you have any leads at all?"

"No. A doctor named Johnathan Flagg might have something to do with it. He owned the house very briefly before my husband's family bought it. Or at least he owned the land. The house is actually a summer cottage, and it was moved to its present location either when this Dr. Flagg owned the land, or when my husband's great-grandparents owned it."

"You know, I see a dentist in Cambridge named Johnathan Flagg. You don't suppose they're related?"

"Oh, I doubt it. That would be too incredible.

There must be hundreds of Johnathan Flaggs in the world."

"Well, I'll ask him anyway next time I see him. I'm overdue for my checkup, so maybe this will be the impetus I need. I can't seem to remember to do anything like that since Heddy died."

"Was it a long time ago?" Eleanor asked carefully. She didn't want to appear nosy, but Mr. Hopstedder seemed rather eager to talk about his wife.

"Three years. I still miss her everyday."

Eleanor paused and then decided to speak. "So do I. I mean, I lost my husband two years ago."

"You?" he asked incredulously. "You're so young!"

"It was one of those sudden things. I've had a very hard time dealing with it," she added, as a way of encouragement for her new friend to keep talking.

"It's been terrible for me," he admitted. "Poor Heddy was sick for a long time, but she never lost her confidence that she would recover. Not till the very end. I think it was such a shock to me, because I had come to believe myself that she would get better. But the doctors were right after all."

"I guess it's always a shock, isn't it, even when you are supposed to be prepared?"

"It sure was for me."

Mr. Hopstedder nodded towards a large orange tabby cat that had suddenly appeared, and was arching its back against the coffee table. "But me and Beezus, we get along just fine, don't we Bee?"

"Oh, you have a cat! So do I. A white one with green eyes, named Jasmine. I love cats!"

"Well, this Mr. Beezus is a pretty independent feller, but he knows when I need a friend and he sticks

172

pretty close to me. Don't you Beezus?" he added as he picked up the cat.

"Beezus is a cute name," Eleanor commented reaching over to pet him.

"His real name is Captain Bradley. But for some reason we started calling him Beezus, sometimes just Bee. Don't know where we got that silly name, but he sure seems like Beezus to me now."

Beezus stretched across his owner's lap and began to purr. Eleanor stood up, smiling.

"It was awfully nice to meet you. I really appreciate your letting me come over to see the painting. It's wonderful!"

"It was my pleasure. But you're not going so soon?"

"Oh, I really should. But I'll keep in touch! If I find out anything interesting about Picknell, I'll be sure to let you know."

"You do that. We're always here."

"Thanks again!"

Mr. Hopstedder walked her to the door, and waved good-bye as she drove away. *What a sweet man*, Eleanor thought to herself. But she admitted to herself guiltily, that it was too difficult to see the pain he was still in after the death of his wife. *He needs a social life!* she told herself. *Perhaps I should invite him over one day, and invite Grace and Miranda...* She laughed at herself. *So, when the shoe's on the other foot, you're not so adverse to people going on to have other relationships after all, are you?* Eleanor pondered the hypocrisy of this, all the way home.

* * * *

173

Gertrude's next letter showed that she and Will had not spent much time at home before traveling again.

August 1, 1893
Grand Camp les Bains
Calvados, France

Dear Lizzie,

Telegrams may be convenient, but there is nothing like a real letter! I received yours yesterday and it was wonderful. All of your letters are very precious to me, Lizzie, especially now that I realize how much of my married life will be spent many miles away from you.

Still, I cannot complain, for life seems like one pleasure after another. We are finally settled here at Grand Camp for the summer season, and although the weather has not been good for painting, it has been a delightful social scene! A number of well-known Parisian writers, musicians and actors are settled here, and Henry Mosler and his family are with us, and we invited young Harry Meakin to join us. Do you remember him from our last summer in Annisquam? He is in France on a scholarship from the Cincinnati Art Museum, and Will is quite fond of him. You know that Will will not take pupils per se, but he has become a mentor for the young man, and the two of them go off and paint together whenever they can. I think that Will feels he is repaying the debt he owes to Robert Wylie, by passing on the tradition of taking a younger artist under his wing. However, I must admit that I do not think that Harry has quite the talent that Will has, but he is a delightful companion and absolutely idolizes Will. So I can't help but like him!

Will and Harry were spending a tremendous amount of time painting a very pretty wheat field just outside of town, and they had a promise from the farmer that the wheat would not be cut until next week. Yesterday they arrived on the site with their easels and paint, only to discover that the farmer had decided he needed to get the wheat in early this year! Oh, you have never seen two more disgusted artists! Neither one of them can paint what they can't see, so both paintings must be abandoned. It took many a sip of sherry last evening to get them back into good humor!

Will's Salon paintings were very well received and he was given an excellent position on the line. We heard from a number of people that he was considered for a medal this year, but the fact that it has been some time since he last exhibited at the Salon kept the jury from awarding it. Why that should make a difference I have no idea - it seems very unfair, but Will just laughs the whole thing off.

When Will is off painting I spend my time with the Moslers and the other guests. We women do a lot of walking; and I go swimming at least once a day. There are many children here and we have picnics and games on the beach. Sometimes I still sketch; but here I must admit something that will shock you - I have taken up embroidery! I finally fell victim to the sewing circle. There are women here who do such beautiful work, that I found myself admiring it and then, before I knew what was happening, being taught how to do it! I am glad, though. I like having an artistic occupation of my own. It gives Will something to admire of mine while I am admiring his paintings!

Tell Ida I love the poem she sent me, it is very

beautifully composed. She is perhaps the real genius of our family! Does she have a copy of Emily Dickinson's poems? All of the Americans over here are talking about her poetry. There are two editions out now, both edited by Thomas Wentworth Higginson. If she does not have a copy I will buy them for her for Christmas this year.

Speaking of Christmas, we will be passing back through Paris on the way to the South this winter, and I would like to pick out something special for you and Mama. Write and tell me what your heart desires! I need an excuse to take advantage of the wonderful shopping in Paris!

As for other news, there is none yet, but we still hope... I have taken your advice, but I do hate this waiting from month to month. I try not to be too disappointed, as I promised you.

Give my love to everyone,

Gertrude

Eleanor immediately knew that the "news" Gertrude was waiting for could only be a pregnancy. She wondered just how long the two of them had been trying, as they had been married for well over four years. Eleanor remembered her own impatience with conception - once she and Bill had decided to have a child, it had seemed like ages until she was actually pregnant. But it had only taken four months. Eleanor realized that if Gertrude had discussed her concerns with Lizzie, that must have been back in May when she saw her in person. But they couldn't have been trying to conceive for too long before that, given Will's illness and long recovery.

She was tempted to reach for another letter, in her eagerness to read about the baby. But for the last time, she suppressed the urge.

10

It was Friday. There were only two more days to get through before her official "date" with Nathan, and Eleanor was determined to keep so busy that she barely had time to think about it. She decided to write to the three museums which had Picknells in their collections, and ask for reproductions. She got Bill's old typewriter out of the bedroom closet, and spent the morning on the task.

Eleanor made herself lunch, and found herself thinking again about Brian Suskind's request for an article. *It really would be wonderful to share Gertrude's story.* She began to take seriously the idea that she should start writing. *But first, I want to know everything I can about Gertrude...*

Eleanor was still thinking about descendants, but there was another, deeper reason for her hesitation. She had a strong conviction of predetermination. It was impossible for her to shake the sense that Gertrude's decisions, made a hundred years ago, should affect her own.

At the same time, she realized she was growing impatient with reading one letter a day. *Why don't I just get it over with and finish the letters?* After a brief argument with herself, weighing the pros and cons, reading them all won out. The biggest con - the last letter - seemed to have somehow become less frightening.

Before she knew it, she was upstairs in her room and holding the last of the packet. She spread the letters out on the bed, in order, and counted. *Seventeen left to go. I wonder if these are all the letters she wrote to Lizzie in these years, or if Lizzie only saved some of them?* she asked herself. *Well, there is no way to know.*

She took a deep breath and began reading. The first letter was a very happy one.

December 15, 1893
Villa des Hortensias
Cap d'Antibes
Alpes Maritimes, France

Dear Lizzie,

It has finally happened! We are going to have a baby!
You will wonder why I did not telegram such momentous news, but I have so much to tell you (and besides, you still have seven months left to wait - I am only about two months along). First of all, I feel fine. A little tired, and sometimes I feel ill, but that is to be expected. The strangest things make me feel sick though. I cannot abide tobacco suddenly, although I always found the odor pleasant before. And certain spices - turmeric of all things - must be avoided at all costs! But overall I feel wonderful - we are both so happy we can hardly stand it! Will has told absolutely everyone, so that complete strangers come up and congratulate me on a regular basis. He will be such a doting father!

Did you notice the return address? We have left town because of a smallpox epidemic. We were all in a whirl about where to go, when suddenly this villa became available, high up the hills above town and safe from the disease. You cannot imagine how beautiful and luxurious our surroundings are now! Our garden is something to see and dream about - roses and hortensias everywhere, palm trees and fig and olive trees too - and our view embraces Antibes and a splendid sweep of the Mediterranean, with Nice on the further edge of the bay, and best and grandest of all, the mighty Alps themselves! The Emersons are nearby, and we are just down the road from the Dracopoli's villa. The weather here is magnificent! Not a single cold day yet; we live with the doors and windows wide open. So you can see that I am basking in sunshine and flowers - I can't imagine a more perfect introduction to the world for our baby!

Last week Dr. Emerson sent to London for the smallpox vaccine and we all "stood up like brave little soldiers" (Will's words) and were vaccinated. I have had no effect from the vaccine at all, but it made Will and Harry and some of the others feel very achy and miserable, although of course it is better than having the disease. Dr. Emerson tells me I must stay out of town for a while longer, however, as now they have the grippe down there terribly. But he need not worry, I have no desire to leave the Cape - we are having such a lovely time! We have tea every Sunday with the Dracopolis, and sometimes Dr. Emerson reads us one of his lectures, and the conversations are always so intelligent and enlightening, and the atmosphere so lovely, I can't imagine why one would ever want to leave. And Will is doing the most inspired painting again! He is quite relieved after getting so little done this summer.

We are already in a flutter about names. If it is a girl, I would like to name her Sophie for Will's wonderful Aunt Sophronia. (She died about two weeks before our wedding, remember?) I love the name Sophie. Will, however, thinks that if it is a girl she should be named after me, but, as you know, I have never liked my name and have no intention of burdening another female with it! As for boys names, I want the baby to be named William, for his father and grandfather, but Will thinks we should name the baby after Papa. And although I love him dearly for that, I still prefer the name William to John. We have managed to agree on a middle name! It will be Ford, for Will's uncle Daniel Sharp Ford, who has been so wonderful to him and to us. If we have a boy and we name him William, we will call him Ford to distinguish him from his father.

So, what do you think? You must tell me all of your opinions, but then you must not hold me to them, as I may take a fancy to the name Agnes, or Sylvester, or who knows what in the next seven months!

Oh, Lizzie, write and tell me that special recipe for tea you drank while you were waiting for Ida and Frank. Was it nice? I remember you drinking it all the time, but I was so young then that I didn't pay the proper attention. Were your confinements hard? (I don't remember, although I should.) Were Mama's? Write and tell me everything you remember so that I will be prepared.

I am so glad I learned embroidery - I am making so many nice baby things! I am feeling very domestic, as you would suppose. Maternity certainly makes you look at the world in a very different light! You would hardly recognize me, for although I still look the same, I am so much more content to just sit and watch the world move around me, instead of always wanting to be the one moving!

I miss you so much, Lizzie. Will has promised that we will come to the States after the baby is born. That will be in July, so perhaps this time next year, when the baby is five or six months old, we will be home. Oh, I hope we are home for the baby's first Christmas! Won't Ida and Frank love having a new first cousin to spoil!

Write to me soon, Lizzie.

With love,

Gertrude

Eleanor was delighted to finally have her suspicions confirmed: Gertrude had a child. The next letter was over a year later:

October 15, 1894
American Art Association
131, Boulevard Montparnesse
Paris, France

Dear Lizzie:

Just a quick note to send you this photograph of Ford. He is now three months old, and is a delightful baby - so sweet and easily soothed. He takes all of our moving around quite in stride - I am amazed at how easily he adapts to new environments. The photographer told me that he was one of the easiest children he has ever photographed; the light did not scare him at all.

As you can see, we are in Paris temporarily before sailing for home. Will and I both felt that a formal, Paris portrait only would do for Ford, and we are introducing him to some of the other wonders of this great city as well. He has already been to see Sacré Cœur, and the Louvre, and Notre Dame. I know you are laughing at me, but we believe he is absorbing an artistic appreciation already!

This letter should reach you long before we do. Will has some business to attend to, and I have some shopping to do, before we can leave. I will telegram with the date we are sailing. If you need to reach us, a telegram or letter to the Art Association on this letterhead will be the easiest way. We have settled in a small pension, but it is a bit cramped and we plan to move as soon as we find something better. Of course, Will still has his studio, so you can write there as well if you wish.

I am so glad to be coming home! Will has decided to spend part of the winter in Florida, which I think is very wise. His health has never been quite right since California, and I dread to think of him spending a winter in New England. But you will have Ford and me with you for a whole season! We will make up for much lost time, Lizzie.

Tell Ida and Frank that they will see their new cousin in person soon!

Much love,

Gertrude

The next letter was again over a year later. It also had once apparently contained photographs, but they were no longer with the letter. Eleanor realized that the photograph she had seen with Gabby must have been one of them. *I must tell Gabby that she was right - the picture was taken in the south of France,* she reminded herself.

December 20, 1895
Villa des Hortensias
Cap d'Antibes
Alpes Maritimes, France

Dear Lizzie,

Will has taken these photographs of me and Ford in our garden, so you can not only see us, but our beautiful home as well. Is it not truly the most beautiful place you have ever seen? I send these to you to entice you to visit - Ida and Frank can stay on their own with the housekeeper, and you and William should come and get away from the winter. You have never had the opportunity to travel abroad - oh, do say you will think about it! I miss you so much!

As you can see, Ford is happy and healthy. He is into everything - Nurse and I have to follow him around constantly to keep him out of mischief! The Dracopoli children help keep him occupied; he follows them around like a puppy dog, and they are very sweet not to get tired of it! Speaking of puppies, Ford has also taken a fancy to the Dracopolis' bulldog, Box. He is a very rare breed belonging to the German imperial family, and he has no bark, but does not put up with nonsense nevertheless, so I am worried that Ford will drive the poor thing to distraction one day. Every chance he gets he is heading down the road to see his friend "Bok." ("Box" is a word he cannot quite pronounce yet.) Thank goodness the Dracopolis are so fond of him!

By the time you receive this it will be Christmas. I sent a box to you last week, with greetings for all of you, and I hope it will arrive in time. I remember last Christmas with such fondness! It seemed that it might be the last Christmas we all spend together, with Ida and Frank so grown and Will and I permanently settled in our villa here. But I do have news - Will has a great many collectors waiting for paintings, so it is not unlikely that we will manage another visit back home this spring. It is very important to me that Ford grow up knowing my sister's family!

Will's career is going so well, Lizzie. Ever since the spring, when he won the medal at the Salon, and Munsey's Magazine declared him the greatest painter of sunshine ever, he cannot paint fast enough for Mr. Avery and all of the collectors. It is a great triumph for him, and so well deserved after all of these years. I am so proud, Lizzie! For years, a few precious admirers have believed that he is one of the great masters; now we see the general public believing it too!

Oh, I must go! Ford is trying to climb up the bookcase again. As soon as Nurse's back is turned he looks for the most dangerous thing he can possibly do and attempts it. I would quite despair of him if I was not so utterly in love with him!

Love to all, and write soon.

Gertrude

Eleanor reached for the next letter, but it was only a note - four lines. But they were four lines that made her heart stop.

October 2, 1896
Villa des Hortensias
Cap d'Antibes
Alpes Maritimes, France

Dear Lizzie,

I am hastily writing to let you know that we are taking Ford to Paris for a consultation. He has become lethargic and feverish, off and on. He has seen local doctors but they seem unable to diagnose the problem. I will write or telegram when I have some more news.

With love,

Gertrude

Eleanor grabbed the next letter.

October 6, 1896
Paris, France

Dear Lizzie,

I assume you received my telegram, but just in case I will tell you again. The doctors think that Ford may have meningitis. They have prescribed medicine, and rest, and we are to pray and hope. Many children survive the disease, and we are determined that Ford shall be among them. It may be a long time before we know what the outcome will be, but we are to take him back to Antibes and make him as comfortable as possible. We are hiring an additional nurse, so that he can have full-time care. I am frightened, Lizzie, but I dare not show it. If you know anything about this disease please write to me, especially if you know children who have survived it.

We will be home again in three days. Ford seems a little better so I am anxious to travel right away, while he has some strength. I will feel so much better when he is home, in his own dear bed.

Love,

Gertrude

Eleanor read the next four letters without stopping for a moment to breathe, or think, but tears began to stream down her face.

December 22, 1896
Villa des Hortensias
Cap d'Antibes
Alpes Maritimes, France

Dear Lizzie,

I was so hoping by Christmas to be able to write you a long letter and give you a reason to rejoice, but all remains the same. He has good days and bad days, and we wait and wait. It has been over two months and our spirits are still good - we <u>still</u> <u>believe</u> all will be well, but the waiting is interminable. It seems as if a great trial has beset us just when everything had seemed so perfect, but that is the way of God, is it not, Lizzie? Perhaps we had grown too used to good fortune, and now must suffer a just turn of humility. I would not say this to Will; he does not believe in a God of such personal intervention; he believes in a God of goodness and light - a power of Nature who is benevolent and beautiful always. When bad things happen he believes it is nothing but an accident, and not God's will. I wish I believed as he did, but I fear that there are transgressions I may have made, and now we are all being made to suffer. How I wish I could talk to Reverend Young! The nearest churches are Catholic, of course, and I do not wish to make matters worse by trying to take comfort there. Do you think I am being too hard on myself? I don't know what I could have done, and yet I think I must have done something to deserve this.

Our friends here have been wonderful, and the letters and cards from home are very comforting as well. Sometimes I wake up in the morning, and it is so beautiful here, that I forget that I am unhappy for a small time, until something shakes me out of my reverie, and I remember that there is a great question yet to be answered. Perhaps it is foolish to love Ford so much, perhaps a wiser mother than myself would have understood that life is a gift, and not a promise, and I would have tempered my love with a strong dose of reality. But I cannot regret my feelings, not for a moment. He has been an angel to me on earth, and if he should die, I know he will be an angel in Heaven who I one day will see again.

I fear this letter will distress you, Lizzie. There is no one else to whom I could ever say any of this, so you must bear with me. You are my rock, Lizzie. I trust you to know me as no one else ever could.

I will telegram again at the New Year, I promise.

With all my love,

Gertrude

February 6, 1897
Villa des Hortensias
Cap d'Antibes
Alpes Maritimes, France

Dear Lizzie,

Ford has taken a turn for the worse. I am at his bedside now, as I write, and he is sleeping peacefully but his breathing is terribly labored. The doctor is here two or three times a day, but there is nothing we can do but wait now and pray. Will has just gone to telegram Dr. Emerson again, in the hope that he may have another suggestion. We live as if time was frozen, even more so than we have in the past months.

My head aches, Lizzie, and I cannot write more.

Gertrude

* * * *

Dear Lizzie,

I cannot tell you that there is any change for the better but while he lives we do not wholly give up hope. I have not dated this because I do not know what day it is, but it is two days after my last letter.

With love,

Gertrude

* * * *

February 17, 1897
Villa des Hortensias
Cap d'Antibes
Alpes Maritimes, France

Dear Lizzie,

We laid our Darling to rest in the little grave-yard overlooking the Mediterranean last Sunday. The funeral services were held at the Villa Dracopoli, the large drawing room was filled with friends, and all around and about him were heaped wreaths, crosses and many designs of the beautiful flowers he so loved in life. Even after all these months of anxiety and those eight days and nights of agony it seems like a horrible nightmare from which we must wake to find him somewhere, in some way.

You must not worry about us, because we are both well and can sleep and eat. Of course there are periods when the anguish seems too great, too monstrous to be borne, but in between there are long hours when there is almost no sensation, a kind of dull pain as though we were under the influence of some narcotic while going over and over all the incidents of the last few months.

Sometime I wish you would find out what the doctors at home think about meningitis - if, as here, they believe that a child is born with a predisposition, sometimes inherited, toward it.

With much love,

Gertrude

Eleanor put down the letters and sobbed and sobbed, as if Gertrude's loss was her own. Memories of her feelings after Bill's death flooded her; she sympathized acutely with Gertrude and Will; but most of all, the knowledge, long repressed, of how very much she loved Peter was almost unbearable. *I am such a fool. I could have lost Peter at any time these past two years by simple indifference, and never realized it was even happening. I must, I must make it up to him before it is too late. I must tell him how I feel, and never, ever let our relationship get so distant again.*

There was no question of reading any more letters. Eleanor spent the rest of the afternoon trying desperately to think of ways to show Peter how she felt, only to discover, as do all who regret past actions, that there was nothing to be done - except begin the long process of never doing it again. Still, she felt she must attempt an apology, and when Peter came home that evening, she tried to put into words something of what she was feeling.

"Peter," she began, as she sat down at the dinner table with him, "there is something I want to tell you. You were right. I haven't been fair to you these past two years. I was so caught up in my own feelings, that I know I didn't spare much room for yours." She hesitated, then went on: "I hope you can forgive me."

Peter's face, naturally cheerful, grew grave. "Mom, there is nothing to forgive. You did what you had to do. I know you love me."

"I do love you so, with all my heart. Do you really know that, Peter?"

Peter paused before answering. "I always knew that you loved me, Mom. But I think you were so caught up in missing Dad, that you sometimes forgot that I loved you, and we still had each other."

"I hope never to make that mistake again, Peter. Life is so short, and so precious, that to ignore the people you love, even for a moment, is a terrible thing to do."

"Don't be too hard on yourself, Mom. You couldn't help being the way you were. And I don't think you'll do it again." A look of concern crossed his brow. "What brought this on, today? Did something happen?"

Eleanor felt a little silly suddenly. "It's just the letters. Gertrude had a son, and he died. It made me think about you."

"Well, I'm glad, I guess. I mean, I'm glad it's nothing more serious than that."

Eleanor was thinking about something Peter had said. "What made you say that you didn't think I'd ever do it again?"

"I don't know. I guess it's because you're different. You're not the same person you were a few months ago. You're re-joining the world. I think you're starting to be happy again."

Eleanor looked at her son gratefully. "I hope to be happy, I really want to. But happy or unhappy, I can still do a better job of showing you how much I love you."

Peter looked down at his plate, embarrassed, but happy. Suddenly he looked up with a sparkle in his eye. "If you really want to show how much you love me," he offered, "you could take me to that new R-rated Schwarzenegger film I told you about."

"Not on your life," Eleanor replied, with a confident parental smile that Peter hadn't seen for a long time.

* * * *

That night, Eleanor had a dream. She was walking along the beach, and up ahead of her, she thought she saw Gertrude walking along too. Gertrude was holding the hand of a little boy, and Eleanor desperately wanted to catch up to them and see Ford. But as she started to run towards them, Gertrude looked back over her shoulder and began to run away, pulling her son along, as if she was frightened. Eleanor sadly gave up her pursuit, and sat down on a rock. Bill was there, and he sat down next to her. "Why is Gertrude afraid of me?" she asked him. "She's not," he replied, "you're afraid of Gertrude." "I am not!" Eleanor began to protest, but Bill said, "You're afraid of lots of things. You know you are." "But I want to talk to her! I have to ask her something!" Eleanor insisted. "Come on with me," Bill said, and he took her hand and began walking her the other way, towards town. "You go in that direction," he suggested, "and you might see her again."

After that the dream changed, and she and Bill were sitting on a bench talking about many things, and when Eleanor awoke later, her impression of the dream was of it being happy. Only later, when she understood Gertrude's story, did she remember that it was Gertrude who had run away from her.

After breakfast the next morning, Eleanor re-read the letters she had read the day before, this time carefully checking the dates. She discovered that little Ford was just under three years old when he died in 1897, and that it was a horrendous year for Gertrude - Will was going to die that year, too.

Eleanor decided that reading to the end would be too depressing a thing to do on the day she was to have her date with Nathan. She wanted to enter the evening in a positive mood. *I'll call Gabby*, she decided. *She'll want to hear about the letters, and she'll help keep me distracted for a few hours.*

Gabby was more than happy to come over, and the two of them made coffee and sat on the back porch talking. Eleanor filled Gabby in on Gertrude and Will's child, and his death, and Gabby was filled with sympathy. "How sad," she said. "It must have been devastating for them."

"They really loved that child, you can tell from the letters. Not that everyone doesn't love their children, of course, but they seem to have been particularly devoted parents. But the worst of it, Gabby, is that Will dies the same year. I haven't gotten to that part yet, but I know he does."

"Oh, how awful for Gertrude! I wonder how one recovers from a blow like that?"

"I'm not sure she does," Eleanor told her, and confided what she knew about the first sentence of the last letter. "I'm not sure what happens to Gertrude."

Gabby was silent for a moment, lost in thought. Then she surprised Eleanor by saying, "Have you ever noticed how much you and Gertrude have in common? I mean, you both were married to older, famous men, who both died young, and you both have sons, although, thank goodness, Peter is fine and healthy."

Eleanor flushed. She had often thought about it, but she was embarrassed to say what those thoughts were leading her to conclude. She decided to plunge ahead with the conversation, because she was dying to know what Gabby made of it.

"There's more than that, even. Gertrude had a brother who died in the Civil War, and she was born after his death. Well, I had a sister who died before I was born. It may seem like a small thing, but that was the thing that struck me as the oddest of all. My family never got over it, so it had a big impact on my life."

"It's like déjà vu, isn't it? Or walking through time," Gabby said.

"Walking through time? What do you mean?"

"Didn't you ever think about reincarnation? Or maybe just destiny? I mean, we still don't know what those letters were doing in your attic, and even if there is a logical explanation for that, why is it that you were the first person to find them, after so many years?"

"I don't know. Do you believe in stuff like that?"

"Oh, absolutely! Believe me, Eleanor, when

you dig around in history you come across lots of strange stories. Did you know, for example, that a number of the houses in Annisquam are haunted? And that a famous clairvoyant, Leonora Piper, was a resident here for many years in the last century? Famous scholars from around the world tried to discredit her, and they never could."

Eleanor was quiet for a moment, getting up the nerve to ask her next question. "Gabby, if there was a connection between me and Gertrude, what do you think the point of that would be? I mean, why do you think I have the letters?" She leaned forward, eager to hear Gabby's answer.

"Well, if I could tell you that I guess I'd be psychic myself!" Gabby laughed. "But it does seem to me," she added, with more seriousness, "that people often learn things from the past. Let's suppose for a moment that you and Gertrude are the same person, reincarnated. Perhaps there is something you are supposed to do, this time, that you didn't do before, or perhaps you did something before that would help you this time. Or, even if you don't believe in reincarnation, maybe God or fate arranged for you to find the letters for a similar reason - that there is a lesson in them."

Eleanor had been holding her breath, in anticipation of Gabby's response, and now she slowly released it. "That's what I think," she said, in a quiet voice. "I would never have admitted it to anyone, but I'm so glad that you noticed it. I feel this connection to Gertrude, something about her is so compelling to me. I just hope I understand the meaning of all this when I get to the end of the letters. I'd hate to think that I never got the message, especially if it's been divinely sent to me," she added, with a grin.

"Well, I suppose the good thing about it is that if you don't get the right message, you'll probably never know it!" Gabby said cheerfully. "I do know a little about the Eastern view of reincarnation, and it's all about learning and doing things better the next time. I suppose you'll just keep coming back again, making all the same mistakes, until you finally get it right."

"Well, I would prefer not to live some aspects of this life over again, if you please. So, believe me, I am going to give this a lot of thought, before I jump to any conclusions."

"In a way," Gabby said thoughtfully, "you've already been influenced positively by the letters. I mean, and I hope you won't mind my telling you this, the talk around town was that you were terribly depressed before you came here. And, well, you don't seem that way anymore."

"No, I'm not. And I don't mind talking about it. I was really depressed, Gabby, and nothing seemed to be able to make me happy. These letters, if nothing else, have given me a much-needed distraction. They got me to stop thinking about myself, and think about other people. Not just Gertrude and all of that, but Peter especially. Even my friendship with you... let's just say that it wouldn't have happened a few months ago. I wouldn't let anyone in; I felt like my life was over, and I'm embarrassed to admit that I didn't even care if it was. It was easier that way, than trying to go on with it."

"I think I can understand how that could happen. It sounds like maybe it happened to Gertrude."

"Maybe."

197

The two women were quiet for a moment, each lost in thought. Gabby was the first to speak.

"Eleanor, whatever happens to Gertrude, remember that you are <u>not</u> her. Even if you are reincarnated, and all of that, you still are not her. You are you, here today."

Eleanor smiled gratefully at her. "How do you know me so well, Gabby? That's just what I was thinking about. And I'm glad you said that, it's important for me to remember that."

Gabby smiled at her, mischievously. "Maybe I know you so well because I'm reincarnated too. Maybe I knew you before. Hey, maybe I'm Lizzie! Or maybe I'm Will!"

They both laughed. "Maybe you are!" Eleanor agreed, adding, "but then, how come I have to be the older one this time around?"

Both women giggled, and then decided, after agreeing to keep this conversation to themselves, that to go down that road was too much, and there were some things they'd rather not know.

* * * *

Miraculously for Eleanor, who had been dreading a day of acute suspense, the day flew by. After Gabby left, Eleanor put on her bathing suit and found Peter and Alan at the beach. Kelly and Rob wandered down soon after, so the adults enjoyed a lively conversation at the edge of the water, while the boys dove under the waves trying to see who could find the most interesting shells. The Smiths invited

Peter and Eleanor to join them for dinner, and, surprisingly, did not press the invitation when Eleanor said she had plans. Eleanor suspected that they already knew she was going to dinner with Nathan, but appreciated their discretion nevertheless.

Eleanor dressed carefully for her date, choosing a floral-patterned skirt with a matching soft pink sweater, and white sandals. She was ready twenty minutes ahead of time and nervously paced the house waiting for Nathan. When she saw him pull into the driveway, she started out the door before he had a chance to come and get her.

She let herself into the passenger seat and smiled at him. He had dressed up as well - tan gabardine pants and a polo shirt in tan and green - and Eleanor's first thought, despite herself, was that he looked great. Immediately she blushed and turned away.

"Tom Shea's okay?" Nathan asked. Tom Shea's was a renowned seafood restaurant in Essex.

"Oh yes. They have great food," Eleanor answered nervously.

As they drove, Nathan talked about the status of Mrs. Conboy's house, some ideas he had for his fall semester students, a little local gossip, and the weather. By the time they arrived at the restaurant, Eleanor was perfectly at ease, and wondering why she'd been so nervous in the first place.

They ordered wine and appetizers, which arrived quickly before the rest of the meal. Eleanor noticed that the restaurant was decorated much as Nathan's dining room, which made them both laugh. "But it's not nearly as well done," she added playfully.

"So, Ellie, tell me the latest about yourself. How are those letters?"

"Well, the latest is that I tried to finish them yesterday. I guess I'm tired of waiting to find out what happens. Anyway, I couldn't get through them all, because Gertrude and Will have a son, and then he dies when he's only two and a half."

"Oh, how sad," Nathan interjected.

"Yes, I have to admit it really affected me. It put me in a funk for the rest of the day. But it made me do some thinking about Peter. Good thinking. I want to be there for him again. I guess you know I really haven't been these past two years."

"Did you tell him that?"

"Yes!" Eleanor was pleased to be able to report. "We had a good talk last night, and I feel so much better, and so does he, at least I think he does."

"That's great!"

"Mmmm. But the letters upset me for another reason as well."

"Why was that?"

"Gertrude's reaction to the whole thing. She blamed herself, at least in one of the letters she did. She felt that God was punishing her. She seemed to think it was some sort of divine restitution because she'd been so happy."

"That's a very Puritan way of looking at things, but not unusual for a New Englander, especially in the nineteenth century. Those old ideas of sin and judgment really die hard."

"There were times when I felt that way too, about Bill. Like God was punishing me. But never to the extent that Gertrude did. I'm not as religious as she seems to have been. I really couldn't keep up the viewpoint that God was purposely making me suffer, maybe because I spent so much time as an adolescent telling myself that death was just an accident. Anyway, I really feel for Gertrude - having to think that she was somehow responsible. It seems terribly unfair."

"She was certainly being unfair to herself. And it sounds unusually dramatic, considering that children died a lot more often last century than they do today. Although I suppose by the end of the century it was becoming rare enough that parents let themselves believe it wouldn't happen to them."

"That's exactly what they did! She and Will absolutely doted on their son, and I think their grief was greater because of it. Plus, the illness went on for months, they had far too much time to think about it."

"Do you know if they had any more children?"

Eleanor sighed. "I haven't read any more than that, but I know they didn't. Will dies the same year. In fact, there are only a few letters left."

"What are you going to do when you get to the end?"

"I don't know. What do you mean?"

"I mean, if you still don't know the answer about why you found the letters in your attic."

"I guess I'll keep digging until I do. But maybe it's a mystery I won't be able to solve. What do you think?"

"I think that with enough determination there is very little you couldn't accomplish, Ellie. So if there's a way to know, you'll find it."

Eleanor smiled in gratitude. "Thank you. You know, you always say the nicest things to me."

"I mean them, Ellie. I don't just say them to hear myself talk, you know! Now, if you don't mind my asking, what did you mean about telling yourself that death was just an accident, when you were a teenager?"

Eleanor told Nathan the story of her sister's death, and her family's behavior. When she finished, Nathan admitted it was a harrowing story. "No wonder you had such a hard time with Bill's death," he commented.

"I suppose it wasn't a very auspicious introduction to the subject. For the longest time, though, I blamed the therapist they sent me to. He made me realize all these difficult things about my family, and I hated him for it. I still don't like counseling - which isn't very productive, given the circumstances."

"You must have had a bad one. Most people walk away from therapy feeling better, not worse."

"Have you ever seen a therapist?"

"No. But I know a lot of people who've benefited from it."

"You know, I knew you were going to say you'd never been to counseling. You're so *healthy*! Really, it's quite sickening," Eleanor added, teasing.

Nathan was serious. "Eleanor, don't see yourself as a walking basket-case. I can assure you that you are not. You are going to be all right, I promise. Better than all right. Extraordinary... remember?"

Eleanor blushed deeply and crumbled a piece of bread into her bread plate. "I don't know what that means..." she began.

"You don't have to know," Nathan interrupted. "Just be yourself, and it will happen."

The waiter chose this moment to bring the main courses - grilled sea bass, and Maryland-style crab cakes. Dinner was consumed while talking of new things: memories of previous years and previous people in Annisquam, and various trips each of them had taken to other parts of the country and the world. They were both quite stuffed by the time the meal was finished, and declined dessert. The waiter brought the bill with coffee, and Nathan handed him a credit card.

When he was signing the bill, Eleanor found herself watching him, absently. Suddenly she grew slightly pale. Nathan had signed the receipt, "Johnathan Lane."

"Your real name is Johnathan?" Eleanor asked.

"Uh-huh. Why?" Nathan asked, looking up. "Is something wrong?"

"No, of course not."

But Eleanor had felt a strange chill as he'd written his name. The name "Johnathan Flagg" had popped into her mind so strongly. She knew, in that instant, that Dr. Flagg was going to be a huge part of Gertrude's story. But if she'd been asked, at that moment, how she knew, she could never have said.

They walked out into the cool summer air, and Eleanor sighed with delight. The whole sky was lit up with stars, and the moon shone off the water behind the restaurant dock. "What a beautiful night!" she exclaimed. Nathan looked at her. "You're beautiful," he said, and before she knew what was happening, he leaned over and kissed her.

"I thought this was just a friendly evening," Eleanor said, with a nervous giggle.

"Is it? I forgot." And he kissed her again.

"Don't Nathan. Don't go so fast," Eleanor protested.

He stepped back from her and smiled. "Okay, I won't. I promise."

But it felt very natural to hold his hand as they

walked back to his car, and Eleanor knew it would not be easy to slow down this relationship, if she wanted to.

Nathan was relatively quiet during the drive home. In her driveway, he apologized for kissing her. "That wasn't fair, was it? I promised you only a friendly dinner, and I crossed the line."

"Well, you needn't feel so bad," Eleanor reassured him. "It's not as if I really believed you only wanted to be friends. I know there's something between us. But I don't want to end up hurting you, Nathan. I'm not ready for this, at least I don't think so."

"Small steps," was his reply. Eleanor looked at him in surprise - those were Grace's words. "Small steps," he continued. We'll take it very slowly, one step at a time."

"Okay. We'll try it that way." They walked to the cottage front door and hugged - a rather platonic hug - and Eleanor whispered "Good night" into Nathan's ear, and then she disappeared inside the house.

* * * *

Eleanor awoke the next morning to the sound of the telephone ringing. Peter was up and grabbed it. "Mom," he called upstairs, "are you awake?"

"Yes. Who is it?"

"Grandma."

"Tell her I'll be right there." Eleanor threw on a robe and ran downstairs. "Hi!" she said, as soon as she put the receiver to her ear.

"Hi Ellie! How are you?"

"Fine, Mom. What's up?"

"Nothing special. I just wanted to hear your voice. Anything new with those letters?"

Eleanor filled Mary in, but glossed over the son's death. She was in a good mood, and didn't want to think about death or grief. "Did you remember anything else that might explain the letters?" she asked her mother-in-law.

"No, but I did have an idea. Why don't you search the rest of the desk? I always thought it was completely empty, and obviously it wasn't. Maybe there's something else in there that will give you a clue."

"I can't believe I didn't think of that!" Eleanor exclaimed. "That's a great idea. I'll do it today."

"Let me know if you find anything. How's everything else?"

"Oh, fine. I had dinner last night with Nathan at Tom Shea's," she stated, as casually as she could.

"How nice," was Mary's only reaction. "Tell him we say hello."

"I will," Eleanor promised. "What's Dad up to?" she asked, changing the subject. The rest of the conversation was focused on life in Florida; they hung up about ten minutes later.

"Peter," Eleanor immediately turned towards him. "Would you like to help me search that old desk in the attic to see if we can turn up any more information?"

"Sure! Hey, we should have thought of that ages ago!"

"I know. It's silly, isn't it. Let's have breakfast

quickly and then head up to the attic."

After a hastily swallowed meal they climbed the stairs to the attic and stood before the desk. Peter asked his mother which drawer had contained the letters. Eleanor pointed to the lower left drawer. "Well, let's check there first," Peter suggested. "Maybe there are more letters crammed into the back." They opened the drawer carefully, as Eleanor warned Peter that it had fallen out before, but found nothing. Peter checked behind the drawer as well, in case something had fallen through the back, but again, nothing was there. Peter continued checking the drawers up the left side of the desk, and Eleanor checked the right side. They both reached the top without finding anything. Only the center drawer was left.

Eleanor pulled it out but didn't see anything, much to her disappointment. Peter, however, stopped her before she closed it again. "Hey, I think there is a little slip of paper caught at the back. Let me reach in and see if I can pull it out."

Peter's arm emerged with an old piece of paper, rather small in size. He smoothed it out on top of the desk and they both began to read. "It's some sort of moving slip," Peter announced. It read as follows:

July 5, 1903
Parsons Moving Company
35 Pleasant Street
Gloucester, Massachusetts

Receipt for:
Dr. Johnathan Flagg
143 Huron Avenue
Cambridge, Massachusetts

Move one (1) desk from #6 Willow Street,
Waltham to Flagg cottage in Annisquam, corner of
Adams Avenue and Highland Avenue.
Total Cost: $15.00

"Is that our cottage, Mom?" Peter asked, confused. "Highland Avenue goes the other way."

"I'm sure it's our cottage," Eleanor replied with excitement. "The whole street used to be referred to as Highland Avenue, before they began calling our section Planter's Neck. And look, Peter, that address in Waltham is Lizzie's address. That means the desk came from her house. She must have forgotten that she'd left Gertrude's letters in there!"

"So this Dr. Flagg bought the desk from Lizzie and then moved it to the cottage?"

"I don't know. That part doesn't make any sense, unless Dr. Flagg is connected to the family somehow. Otherwise, it's too much of a coincidence that he just happened to own the cottage where Gertrude spent her summers, and just happened to buy a desk from Lizzie Johnson, her sister. There must be a lot more to the story. One thing this does prove, though, is that Dr. Flagg is the one who moved the cottage. He bought the land in January of 1903, and then the cottage was moved here before July."

"Mom, you should drive down to Cambridge this week and check out this address. Maybe the Flagg family still lives on Huron Street."

"Peter, it was an awfully long time ago. It's very unlikely that this address will still be in the family."

"Well, maybe someone else on the street will

know something about the Flagg family. It's worth a shot!"

"You're right, it is. I'm going to finish the letters today, and I'll go to Cambridge tomorrow. In the meantime, thanks for helping me with this. I wouldn't have found that piece of paper without you!"

"Hey, my pleasure, Mom. Anytime."

Peter gave Eleanor an idea of his itinerary for the day, and he soon left to meet up with Alan. Eleanor phoned Mary to tell her about their discovery, then she carried the moving receipt to her bedroom, settling in to read the rest of the letters.

Immediately she knew that the part of Gertrude's story she'd been dreading the most was imminent.

May 15, 1897
Paris, France

Dear Lizzie,

Will is ill. He can't seem to shake a persistent cough and general lethargy. We came up to Paris to see the Salon exhibition, and the change of scenery and seeing his many friends seems to have helped, but I have decided that we are coming home anyway. I know that I need to see you all, and Will needs to be among his family as well. I have written to the Fords, and we are going to their house in Marblehead, where Nellie, Minnie and George will join us. We sail in three days. I will come to you as soon as I settle Will in Marblehead. Don't worry, Lizzie, I am well, and I feel confident that the love and care of family will help Will get well again - I fear that depression may be more of a cause than any true disease.

With all my love,

Gertrude

Eleanor shook her head. It was hard to pick up the next letter.

* * * *

July 10, 1897
c/o Daniel Sharp Ford
Highland Court
Marblehead, Massachusetts

Dear Lizzie,

Thank you for visiting me. I could not leave Will's side, but your visit meant so much to me. He is much better. The love and care of family seems to be having an effect. Will is talking about a trip up to Boston to see Saint-Gaudens' Shaw Memorial on the Common. I am hoping we will be able to go in about two weeks. The doctor has to give his permission before we can travel, but he assures me that it is only a matter of days.

With love,

Gertrude

* * * *

August 7, 1897
c/o Daniel Sharp Ford
Highland Court
Marblehead, Massachusetts

Dear Lizzie,

My hand shakes as I write this. The doctor has just left. There is nothing more anyone can do. I am trying not to panic, and thank goodness Nellie and Minnie are here. They are so calm. I can barely think.

Lizzie, he seemed so well just a week ago! How can this be happening? The doctor says his heart has been weak ever since California, but he seemed so well for so many years! He was perhaps never as robust as before that, but we never dreamed he was in any danger! The doctor thinks that the dual blow of his mother and son passing away this year is just too much for his system. Why doesn't he fight for me, Lizzie? I can't bear to think of life without him!

Oh Lizzie, how can I tell you what horrible thoughts I torture myself with. Does he not love me enough to stay alive for my sake? I have stayed alive for his! I could have given in to despair when we lost Ford, but I would never leave him. Oh Lizzie, help me to banish these thoughts! They are too cruel, too unfair. I know he loves me, and yet, I can't live without him, I don't know what to do.

I feel as if I am going mad. Perhaps you had better come to me again - I think I am not well.

Gertrude

Poor Gertrude, Eleanor thought. *She doesn't really blame him for his death,* Eleanor knew from her own experience, *she's just so distraught.* Eleanor felt slightly ill - she didn't want to go through Gertrude's grief with her - but she forced herself to keep reading.

> *August 12, 1897*
> *c/o Daniel Sharp Ford*
> *Highland Court*
> *Marblehead, Massachusetts*
>
> *Dear Lizzie,*
>
> *Thank you for sending Dr. Flagg to me.*

(*There he is!* Eleanor thought in triumph. *Now we will get to the bottom of this.*)

> *I spoke with him for three hours. He was very kind and patient with me, and gave me some helpful advice. I do feel much better, as you said I would. He gave me a sedative to take if I can't sleep, for he believes that good sleep is the key to coming out of a shock. I hope he will be right.*
> *The petition to administer Will's estate was submitted today. The Justice assured me that it would be granted, but that it might take up to a month to receive the official reply. In the meantime, I am arranging for Ford's body to be sent to Woodlawn, so he can be buried next to his father.*
> *Cards and letters have been pouring in. The Museum of Fine Arts, and the Saint Louis Museum too, have contacted me about a retrospective exhibition. I am so glad! Will would be very pleased.*

I think I will go home with Nellie and Minnie for a while, back to Boston. They have been wonderful.

With love,

Gertrude

P.S. I've been meaning to tell you how much I appreciate all that you and Ida did for me. I love you both so much.

* * * *

October 5, 1897
54 The Fenway
Boston, Massachusetts

Dear Lizzie,

I have, gratefully, been so busy that there is little time to grieve. Both the Saint Louis exhibition and the one here in Boston are taking up most of my time. There are many details to see to, and everything must be perfect for Will's sake. Dr. Emerson has agreed to write a biographical note for the Boston show. I am so glad, as he knew and loved Will with all his heart.

I will not go to Saint Louis, although they have offered to pay my way. The exhibition there will open in December and last about one month, then the paintings will be shipped back to the Fine Arts Museum. I am borrowing a number of his best works for the Boston show, so that altogether there will be about forty paintings.

Nellie and Minnie have been suggesting that I donate some of Will's works to museums, to help ensure his reputation. But I cannot part with the best ones, yet. Mr. Avery wrote me asking about an estate sale. I think I may do that, Lizzie. It will put many good paintings out in public hands, and allow me to keep the rest until I die. Then I will leave those to museums in my will.

I feel as if I must do all this quickly, as I fear that I do not have long to live. I am not sick, dear Lizzie - it is more a presentiment I have. Please do not be alarmed. Perhaps it is only the foolish workings of an overwrought mind. I do not know, but part of me yearns to be with Will and Ford. When I have finished with the exhibitions, and the sale, what will there be to live for? I dare not think of it.

I am not making much sense, I know. I am tired, and will write again soon.

Love,

Gertrude

* * * *

November 1, 1899
54 The Fenway
Boston, Massachusetts

Dear Lizzie,

I have decided to move Will and Ford to Mount Auburn cemetery.

(My goodness, this is the third time she's buried that child!, Eleanor realized.)

I have purchased a plot big enough for the three of us, as well as Nellie and Minnie and George. Nellie and Minnie have convinced me that an artist of Will's stature must be buried at Mount Auburn.
The new interment will be on the 11th in the morning. There will be a small ceremony, and then luncheon at home. I will see you then.

With love,

Gertrude

* * * *

January 20, 1900
The Plaza Hotel
New York, New York

Dear Lizzie,

Everything sold yesterday! Although some people felt the paintings did not always fetch their worth, it was very heartening to see all of the paintings sell. Most of the works sold for under $500, but "In California" sold for over $2,000! How Will and I both loved that painting! Mr. Avery very kindly gave me my choice of the paintings to keep, even though the catalogue for the sale had already gone to press. I have my portrait back, and a number of *other works with particular memories. I had forgotten about some of the paintings that Mr. Avery still had - when he began bringing them out of storage, I was quite overwhelmed by the number of them!*

So many dear friends and well-wishers attended the sale. I did not feel nearly as sad as I thought I would. Rather, it was so wonderful to see how much Will's work is appreciated! I know that Will was watching from heaven, and I am sure he was pleased.

Dr. Flagg sent a very nice note to me just before the sale. He urges me to come see him again when I return to Boston. I think I will. He has been very helpful, I think.

With love,

Gertrude

There was only one left. The last letter. Eleanor slowly took it out of the envelope. As she unfolded it, she made a promise to herself. *I will not rest until I find out how these letters came to be in the attic.* Then, with a great sense of purpose, she began to read.

January 13, 1903
54 The Fenway
Boston, Massachusetts

Dear Lizzie,

Ever since Will died, my life has been meaningless. For the past five years I have been existing, but not living. I do not want to live, yet it seems to be my fate that I do not get sick and die. I go on, day after day, with no purpose other than to keep Nellie and Minnie company.

You know that Dr. Flagg has been visiting me often. I believed his interest in me was purely professional. Yesterday I had a shock. He has asked me to marry him. He says that he loves me, and I believe him, although until he said so I had never given the matter any thought.

Johnathan (for I suppose I must call him that after a marriage proposal) says that I need to go on with my life. He says he will provide me with a reason to live - he speaks of children and a future which I cannot imagine. There is no question that he is kind and will be good to me. He has been good __for__ me, as you have often pointed out. But I do not love him.

216

Is it right to marry someone I do not love? Do you think I will grow to love him, as he says I will? I feel incapable of deciding this for myself. Lizzie, I will abide by whatever you say. I believe you will know better than myself what I should do.

I should tell you that Johnathan has purchased land in Annisquam, up on Highland Avenue, next to where the twin was moved. He intends to buy our cottage from the Langdons and place it there. He does this, he says, to prove that he is not afraid of my past, but understands that I have feelings I will always cherish, and he wants me to know I can have both a past and a future with him. I admit I was very moved by this, but I also fear he took a great gamble in buying the land without knowing my response.

What do you think of this, Lizzie? I told Johnathan I would give him my answer in a week, and he has agreed not to press the issue, if I refuse him.

With love,

Gertrude

Eleanor sat on her bed in quiet amazement. *Dr. Flagg asked her to marry him! He did move the cottage, but he owned the land for only two years. Did she marry him?* All sorts of possibilities were going through Eleanor's head. Perhaps they married, but later found they didn't want the past (in the form of the cottage) after all. Perhaps he moved the cottage but never won her hand. Perhaps they married and lived happily ever after, and Gertrude grew to love him. Or perhaps they married and Gertrude never grew to love him. Eleanor shuddered. *I would have advised her not to marry him,* she decided. *But did Lizzie?*

Eleanor's head was spinning, and she was dying to share her latest findings. She was gratified to discover that it was still early afternoon, and the sun was shining brightly. *I feel as if I've been in a tunnel, all dark and narrow,* she realized, and eagerly headed out the door.

As she walked through town, the sea air and sunshine raised her spirits. She began to look at Gertrude's last letter in a whole new light. *Why, it's perfectly possible that she married him and was happy,* she told herself. *I don't know why I had such a negative reaction to the idea. Why shouldn't she have married him and had more children and lived a long and happy life?*

But at the same time, a voice was nagging at the back of her mind. *Of course she didn't,* it scolded. *She couldn't love anyone else. She had only one true love, and that was Will.*

Eleanor found herself on Leonard Street in front of Grace's home. She wandered up the driveway and knocked on the front door. Miss Wilkins let her in, and ushered her into the sunroom. There she found Grace and Lydia, deep in conversation. But they both looked up with pleasure as Eleanor entered the room.

"Ellie! What a nice surprise. I was just trying to fill Lydia in on what you had told me about those letters you found, but I think I'm getting the story mixed up. Sit down and help me!"

Eleanor was glad to oblige. "I was just coming to tell you the latest. I don't know what to think of it." She sat down, breathless. And she quickly brought the two older women up to date.

"She must have married him," Lydia concluded. "Otherwise, why would he have moved the desk?"

"It does seem that way. But she was so apathetic about the whole thing! I wonder what Lizzie told her."

"It sounds as if Lizzie introduced them in the first place," Grace noted, "So I would think she would support the idea of their marriage."

"Yes, but you must remember that she seems to have introduced him as a doctor, not a suitor. He did cross the line, don't you think?"

"I don't know. Not necessarily. You said there were almost six years between their first meeting and his proposal. By the time he proposed she may no longer have been under his medical care. In which case she should have been alerted to the fact that he still came to see her."

"Perhaps. It's impossible to know, isn't it?" Eleanor turned to Lydia. "Lydia, how can I find out if they ever married?"

"Massachusetts vital statistics. It shouldn't be that hard, since you know the year and their names."

Lydia gave Eleanor directions to the state records in Boston. "I think I'll go tomorrow," Eleanor announced. "I was going to go to Cambridge to check out the address on the moving label, but that is really a long shot, isn't it?"

Lydia shrugged. "You never know. You could check the phone book too. Look up all the Flaggs. Or any of the other names. You might get lucky!"

"Do you really think that could work?" Eleanor asked, surprised that an idea of such simplicity might be fruitful.

"I once found a long-lost cousin that way," Lydia told her. "Simply got out the phone book and started calling. Tracked him down in a matter of minutes."

Eleanor bounded out of her chair. "I can't stand it, I have to go home and check right now. Sunday is a good day to call, isn't it? People tend to be home."

"Well, dear, go to it," Grace encouraged. "Let us know what you find out!"

As Eleanor was walking out of the room she heard Lydia lean over and say to Grace, "I should have told her the rest of the story about that cousin. He turned out to be a shocking disgrace to the family...." Eleanor laughed all the way down Grace's driveway.

When she arrived back at the cottage she headed straight for the kitchen and grabbed the greater Boston directory from the cabinet next to the telephone. She spread it out on the kitchen table and began searching. First she looked for a descendant of Nellie, Minnie or George, but there were no Picknells listed at all. There were four columns of Powers, but that was the least likely name to yield information, as Gertrude and Lizzie had no other living siblings. As for Johnsons, there were seven pages of them! Finally she turned to the Flaggs.

There were a dozen of them. One was a dentist in Cambridge - Mr. Hopstedder's dentist apparently. All the other Flaggs lived in and around the Boston area, but not in Cambridge. She decided to call the dentist first.

The phone rang four times and then an answering machine picked up. She decided not to leave a message - she didn't know what in the world she would say. But she quickly dialed Mr. Hopstedder's number. He had said he'd be calling the dentist to make an appointment - perhaps he knew something.

Samuel Hopstedder was very pleased to hear

from her. "Mrs. Strayer," he began, before she'd even stated why she was calling, "I was going to call you tomorrow night. I'm going to see that dentist tomorrow. I'll ask him if he knows anything about Picknell or your Gertrude."

"Oh thank you! That was just what I was calling about. I found out that Gertrude got a marriage proposal from that Dr. Flagg, and I'm hoping to find out tomorrow at vital statistics whether or not they were actually married."

"Well, I should be home from the city about five o'clock. I'll call you first thing!"

Eleanor hung up the phone and began dialing the other Flaggs in the phone book. She reached four of them, and after bumbling out an introduction managed to get her question across, but none of the Flagg families she reached had any information for her, or even any idea who William Lamb Picknell was. She decided to try the other Flaggs later, perhaps after Mr. Hopstedder talked to his dentist. She couldn't help hoping that the dentist would end up being a descendant - after all, he actually lived in Cambridge.

By late the next morning Eleanor was on her way to Boston. Unfortunately, she discovered upon arrival that the registry of vital records was closed between twelve and two p.m., and it was just about noon. She decided to drive to the public library and kill time, but was too excited to sit and read. After a while she gave up and left the library, deciding to walk up and down Newbury Street and look in the shops.

There were craft stores, boutiques and a number of galleries, but most of the painting galleries were contemporary. However, she knew that Vose Galleries handled historical works only, so she decided to stop in just to see if they had a Picknell painting.

The young woman at the front desk told her to wait a minute while she went to get one of the Vose brothers. After a moment Bill Vose emerged from his office, grinning and holding out his hand for her to shake.

"Haven't you been in before?" he asked, indicating that she seemed familiar.

"My husband and I used to come in about once a year, but it's been ages," she admitted.

"Well, what can I help you with today?"

"Do you have any paintings by William Lamb Picknell? I've developed an interest in his work."

"We do!" Bill Vose exclaimed. "We have two of them. If you don't mind following me downstairs, I'll pull them out for you."

They descended to the lower level of the gallery, and Mr. Vose went into a closet and emerged with a landscape of a pumpkin patch at harvest time. Corn shocks mingled with orange flashes of gourd, and a broad sunset across the sky reflected back the warm tones of the fruit. "That one was painted in the 1870s," the gallery owner told her. "Early in Picknell's career."

He went into another room and emerged with a beach scene. Eleanor recognized the view in the painting. "That's painted from Wingaersheek, looking back towards Annisquam," she told him. "I live right up that hill." She pointed to a spot in the middleground of the painting.

"Really? We figured it had to be Annisquam but we weren't certain."

"Oh yes. It's remarkable how little it has changed!"

The painting was one of Picknell's "glare

aesthetic" works - dazzling sunshine reflected off the sand, and the cool greens of the Annisquam hills softened the heat emanating from the scene. "It's gorgeous," Eleanor said.

"It's a beauty, all right. Shall I wrap it up for you?" he added, with a mischievous grin.

Eleanor smiled back and sighed. "I wish you could. But I doubt I can afford it!"

Bill Vose told her the price, and Eleanor apologized for wasting his time. "I had no idea his works brought that much money!" she exclaimed.

"Well, no need to apologize, I'm glad to show them to you. We like to see people in here who appreciate good paintings!"

As they walked back upstairs together, Mr. Vose suggested that she get on their mailing list, so she could be notified if they got any more Picknell paintings. "I'm happy to keep you informed," he told her. "You never know when you'll win the lottery and want to come back and buy a painting!"

Eleanor thanked him, laughing, and gave her name and address to the receptionist before she left.

She had just enough time to grab a sandwich before heading back to the records registry. Once inside, she was asked to sign in, and was directed to the index tables. There she found the volume for 1903, and looked up Johnathan Flagg. In a moment she had discovered that yes, Gertrude Powers Picknell and John S. Flagg had married.

Eleanor stood staring at the entry for a moment, then jotted down the date, volume and page number so she could fill out a request form to see the actual record. There was a fairly long line waiting for the research assistants, but when she reached the front, it only took a minute for the staff person to retrieve what she wanted. Eleanor was handed a role of microfilm and directed towards an empty reader. Within minutes she had all the available details on the wedding. She copied them down and then left the building.

The city was bustling with summer tourists. Eleanor found a bench and sat down to think. She was strangely disappointed. Part of her had wanted Gertrude to remain Picknell's wife, in heart and soul and legally, forever. But, she realized, that wish had more to do with her own life than Gertrude's. She had been struggling to remain true to Bill forever, and now, with this new information about Gertrude, she could feel her own ideas about love and marriage being given another jolt. *Still, maybe she never did love Johnathan Flagg*, she thought to herself, and then felt instantly ashamed. That was a terrible thing to wish for - it would mean so much unhappiness for Dr. Flagg.

Eleanor found herself thinking about Nathan, and what she was doing to him. *I shouldn't see him if I really can't enter into the relationship fully*, she warned herself. But she knew one thing for certain - she would never marry a man she did not love.

* * * *

When Eleanor arrived home, she heard the phone ringing as she entered the cottage. She ran to pick it up. "Yes?" she inquired into the receiver, out of breath.

"Mrs. Strayer! You are finally home! I have big

news for you!" It was Samuel Hopstedder.

"Tell me! What happened at the dentist?"

"Turns out my dentist is your Mr. Flagg's nephew. Knew all about Gertrude and Picknell! He wants to meet you."

"When?"

"As soon as possible. Call him tonight. Here's his number."

Eleanor jotted it down. "I'm so excited, I can't believe it! Finally, a relative! Did he tell you anything about them? Did they have children? Dr. Flagg and Gertrude, I mean."

"No...," Mr. Hopstedder hesitated for a second. "Actually, he acted a little strange about it. He was anxious to see you, but he said he thought it was odd that you would be interested in Gertrude. Didn't quite know what he was thinking."

"Well, I'm sure he'll explain it when I see him. It probably took him by surprise, that's all."

"Maybe you're right. Now, promise you'll call me after you see him! I want to know all about it."

"I will, Mr. Hopstedder. And thank you so much!"

"No problem. Just glad to be of help."

Eleanor hung up the phone and immediately dialed the dentist. "Dr. Flagg? This is Eleanor Strayer. I believe Samuel Hopstedder told you about me."

"Yes! What exactly is your interest in my aunt Gertrude?" Dr. Flagg's voice was demanding and a touch defensive, as if he was suspicious of Eleanor's motives.

Eleanor explained all about the letters, and about not knowing what happened to Gertrude after the marriage. When Dr. Flagg spoke again, he sounded much more gracious.

"I can see that there is a lot you don't know. Why don't you come by the house on Wednesday afternoon, after my office hours. Say, three o'clock?" He gave Eleanor directions to his home in Lexington. "The Cambridge address is only my office," he explained.

All day Tuesday, Eleanor was bouncing off the walls in restless expectation. She couldn't bear to be cooped up indoors, so she spent the day visiting. First she stopped by the Conboy house to fill Nathan in on the latest (although Peter had actually beaten her to it), then she visited both Grace and Gabby to bring them up-to-date. She even stopped at Lydia's home, to thank her for both the vital records information, and the phone book idea. "Although, isn't it an amazing coincidence that Mr. Hopstedder's dentist is a descendant of the right Flagg family?" she asked Lydia.

Lydia shrugged in her characteristic way. "Life is full of coincidences. Haven't you noticed that yet, Ellie? But I'm glad you are going to find the answers you've been looking for. Now you'll know for certain why the letters were in your cottage."

When Wednesday afternoon finally arrived, Eleanor was so excited that she had to remind herself to concentrate on her driving all the way to Lexington. She pulled into the driveway of a 19th century white Victorian home, trimmed in black, elegant and neatly kept. As she rang the doorbell she could feel her heart pounding.

The door was opened by an elderly gentleman wearing a blue Oxford button-down shirt and linen pants. He had a thin, distinguished face and a no-nonsense air about him, but he smiled and shook

Eleanor's hand and seemed glad to see her.

Immediately upon entering the living room Eleanor's eye was drawn to a large portrait over the fireplace. It was a scene from a cluttered drawing room, where a young woman with red hair was playing a piano - her body turned so that her profile was only partly visible. Glittering on her left hand was a diamond ring and matching wedding band, and spread along the floor behind her was a bear rug - complete with nails and teeth. "That's Gertrude, isn't it?" she asked her host. "It's a portrait she talks about in one of the letters."

"Yes, that's Gertrude. My uncle once told me that Picknell didn't think he could paint Gertrude's face well enough, so he put her in that position so he didn't have to. She left my uncle that portrait in her will. It's the only thing she left him."

Something about that last sentence gave Eleanor a start, and she turned a questioning face to Dr. Flagg. "I don't know much about their relationship," she began hesitantly. "I have a feeling, though, that there is something you wish to tell me."

"Perhaps you'd better sit down. Can I get you anything? Tea? Coffee?"

Eleanor declined and sat down on the edge of the sofa, expectantly. Dr. Flagg cleared his voice and then began.

"You might think it odd that I was not initially eager to see you. You see, no one in this family likes to talk about Gertrude. She hurt my uncle very deeply."

Eleanor sucked in her breath. "What happened?" she asked.

"Well, you know, I guess, that Gertrude was very attached to her first husband."

Eleanor nodded.

"It seems," Dr. Flagg continued, "that she didn't love my uncle when she married him. But he was crazy about her." A smile played upon the dentist's face for a moment. "I remember my uncle talking about her. He would talk about her for hours, if you let him."

"He was her doctor, I believe?"

"Yes. He met her just after Picknell's funeral. He was her sister's family doctor, and he had a reputation for being something of a specialist in nervous disorders. Lizzie, Gertrude's sister, thought that she needed medical attention because she was so distraught, so she arranged for my uncle to go and see her. That was in 1897. He always said he fell in love with her at first sight."

"She never knew that."

"You're right. He courted her for almost six years, and he once admitted that all that time she was apparently quite unaware of his intentions. She was very depressed, but she did seem better when she was in his care, so he naturally came to believe that he was good for her."

"She said as much in her letters."

"Well, anyway, he managed to convince her to marry him. She was gracious, and polite, but she obviously never really recovered from her first husband's death, and the death of her son. My uncle never saw her grow one iota happier. When she died, the family thought it was a blessing."

"She died?" Eleanor asked, taken aback.

"Two years after their marriage."

"Oh." Eleanor absorbed this for a moment, then asked, "What did she die of?"

Dr. Flagg looked pained. "I think there is something you should read," he said. He walked over to a credenza against the wall and opened the top, pulling out a large folder. He brought it back over to the coffee table and began searching the folder for something particular. Finally, he handed her a letter.

The letter was in Gertrude's handwriting, although the writing was sloppy, as if she had had trouble holding the pen. It was addressed to Lizzie in Waltham, and dated June 21, 1905.

Dear Lizzie,

You must excuse my writing. It is hard to write because I have the chills. But there is something I must tell you because I don't want you to blame John.

I am going to die, Lizzie. Please do not be sad. I am so happy to finally be going to Ford and Will. I know that God wants me to die now because he has sent me a sign. I have developed meningitis, just as Ford had. I thank God for this sign, because now I know it is all right to give up the fight.

John has been very angry with me because I refuse to eat or drink or take any medicines. He cannot understand wanting to die. But he should know that this is my dearest wish, and stop trying to change me. I have never lied to him about how I feel.

You must comfort him, Lizzie, after I am gone. I am sure he will meet someone else and go on with his life. He should never have married me, but I think he will be much happier now.

I am only sad to be parting from you, Lizzie, but you are strong and will understand. Tell William and Ida and Frank how much I love them. I will see you all in heaven.

Gertrude

Eleanor looked up, stunned. Dr. Flagg was looking at her hard. "She basically committed suicide. According to my uncle, there was no reason she couldn't have recovered from the typhoid fever. She just wouldn't eat or drink or take anything for it. She ran a high fever for four weeks, and was in and out of delirium. It was a long, painful, and needless death."

"The letter says she died of meningitis," Eleanor stated, confused.

"It's a rare complication of typhoid fever. Gertrude heard it was a possible side effect, and became convinced she had it. My uncle never even believed she did. She wanted to have meningitis, as the letter indicates."

"How did you end up with this letter?" Eleanor asked, still dazed.

"Well, if you received a letter like that from your sister, you'd probably do what Lizzie did. She came running over to their home with it, hoping to convince John to put Gertrude in the hospital and force-feed her. But it was too late. Gertrude had died minutes before she arrived. My uncle should never have read the letter, but he saw it in Lizzie's hand and had it before she could stop him. In the end it stayed with him."

Eleanor was silent for a few moments. Finally, she spoke. "I don't even know what to say to you. I had no idea it ended this way."

"I knew you didn't. That's why I agreed to see

230

you."

Eleanor sat looking at Gertrude's portrait. After a while she asked, "What happened to your uncle? Did he remarry?"

"No, he did not. He was devastated." Dr. Flagg gave Eleanor that hard look again, and then went on. "He became an alcoholic. After a while, he lost his medical license, and after that, he really couldn't live on his own. He came to stay with my mother and me when I was a child, and she took care of him for the rest of his life. He lived to be ninety-six, and he never got over Gertrude's death."

Eleanor took a deep breath. "I'm so sorry. How terribly, terribly sad."

Dr. Flagg looked at her more kindly. "It's an old story. Even I'm surprised at how much it's still an open wound. It's been almost one hundred years since Gertrude died, and the family's still angry with her. We should get over it, shouldn't we?"

Eleanor gave him a weak smile but didn't respond.

"To that end," Dr. Flagg continued, "I think you should have this." He pushed the folder across the coffee table to her. "There are some things in there that will interest you."

Eleanor opened the file and saw that it contained a number of documents - an original marriage certificate for Johnathan and Gertrude; Gertrude's death certificate; Gertrude's will. Also photographs of Gertrude in which she was never smiling, and a photograph of Gertrude and John that must have been a wedding portrait.

Eleanor looked up at Dr. Flagg in surprise. "Are you sure you want me to have these?"

"I don't want to be the keeper of bad memories anymore. You take them. Maybe you can find some sense in Gertrude's behavior. We never could."

"I wish I could say something to you, something helpful."

"It's not your responsibility to defend Gertrude, Mrs. Strayer. From what I understand, you only know about her because of a fluke of chance."

Eleanor wanted to tell him that she thought it was far, far more than a fluke of chance, but she realized the absurdity of trying to explain herself. So she stood up, preparing to leave. Then she thought of one more question she wanted to ask.

"I guess I can assume that your uncle did buy our cottage in Annisquam for Gertrude, and he did have a desk moved from Lizzie's house to the cottage. But do you have any idea why the letters were in there?"

"That's an easy one," Dr. Flagg surprised her by answering. "Just before she married my uncle, Lizzie gave Gertrude back all the letters she had received from her over the years. At least the ones that had been saved. She thought it would be a nice keepsake for Gertrude. I'm sure Lizzie ended up regretting that decision, because Gertrude became quite obsessed with the letters, she read them everyday. One day they disappeared, and she was apparently very upset about it for quite some time. My uncle admitted to me, years later, that he took them and hid them, because he couldn't stand seeing her so caught up in the memories. By the time he told me the story, he no longer remembered where he'd hidden them. Now we know."

"You must have been very close to your uncle."

232

"Well, I was named after him. And I was his confidant. It was easier for him to tell his woes to a child, I think. Too many adults thought he should just get on with his life. Turns out he wasn't that different from his wife, after all."

Eleanor shook her head. Dr. Flagg walked her to the door. "Thank you for seeing me," Eleanor told him. "I really appreciate getting this information."

"Don't let this bother you too much, Mrs. Strayer. It was a long time ago. As I said, it's time to get over it."

Eleanor said good-bye and walked slowly to her car. She sat in the driveway long after Dr. Flagg had closed the door. She was drained. And she didn't know what to think.

Gertrude had done what Eleanor had always believed true love required. She had been true to her death. A needless, hurtful death. A death that left one man, a whole family, devastated. It no longer looked very noble.

Eleanor's head began to hurt. *What does it mean?* she demanded to herself. Then, *Gertrude, what am I supposed to think of this?*

Eleanor picked up the folder that Dr. Flagg had given her. She took out Gertrude's will, and scanned it quickly. It was mostly about paintings - which institutions and people were to get Will's best works - and then one final blow to Johnathan Flagg - she asked to be buried with her first husband.

Mount Auburn Cemetery was on the way home. Eleanor found herself driving there almost by instinct. When she arrived, she was directed to a plot on Orient Path, where she was informed she could find all the Picknells.

The plot was large, centered by an imposing stone monument that simply said "Picknell" on the front. On the reverse were three names and dates:

William L. Picknell
1853 - 1897
Gertrude Picknell Flagg
1864 - 1905

Their son
William Ford Picknell
1894 - 1897

Eleanor kneeled down on the grass and stared at the names. Then she began talking to Gertrude.

"If you only knew, really knew, what you were doing, I know you wouldn't have. I know you never meant to hurt anyone. You simply loved Will and Ford too much. But you never learned anything, Gertrude, you never lived again. You owed them that. They didn't want you to die, I'm sure of it. I'm sure they never wanted you to die for them."

She sat on the grass for a long time, silently thinking. When she finally stood up, she seemed to have come to a resolution.

"Thank you," she whispered, and touching the stone gently, she turned and walked away.

13

The first thing Eleanor did when she got home was call Nathan. He was surprised and pleased.

"Nathan," she announced, "I want to take you to lunch on Saturday."

"Thanks. I'd love to. Want me to pick you up?"

"Nope. I'm driving you in the truck. Come over about noon, and come prepared for a serious conversation."

"Now I'm nervous. Can I ask what about?"

"Well, about us of course. Don't be nervous! Just be prepared to listen."

Next she called Mr. Hopstedder. She knew he'd be waiting to hear from her. She filled him in on the basics, but left out much of the details - only telling Samuel that Gertrude had died two years after the marriage. Eleanor figured that if Dr. Flagg had wanted Mr. Hopstedder to know more than that, he would have told him himself.

Before she hung up, she asked Mr. Hopstedder to reserve the Sunday after next for a small get-together she was planning.

Peter came home and was pleased to hear about a party being arranged. "Just like old times," he declared.

"You can invite anyone you wish," she informed him. "How about Nathan?" he asked, with a sly grin.

"I'm going to invite him myself, smart aleck," his mother retorted.

Grace, Lydia, Miranda and her family were all invited to the upcoming party over the course of the next few days. Eleanor told each one separately what she had discovered in Lexington, but she only poured out her true feelings to Grace.

"It was such a shock, learning about Gertrude's death."

"I bet it was. Killing herself like that, and leaving that poor doctor so miserable. It's a very sad story."

"Yes, but Grace, I could really relate to what she was feeling. It would have been so easy for me to do the same thing! Why, if I hadn't come here this summer, maybe I would have gone on for years and years, being unhappy. Maybe I would have taken the first opportunity out, and just let myself die."

"I don't think so, Ellie. You had Peter to live for. And besides, I don't think you're as much like Gertrude as you think. You always wanted to be happy, you just needed to be shown how."

"Do you think so, Grace?"

"Absolutely." Grace hugged her. "You're going to be fine, now, Ellie. Isn't the world a wonderful place?"

"It is!" Eleanor started laughing and crying at the same time. "Oh, Grace, I don't know why I'm crying! It's ridiculous..."

"No it isn't, Ellie," Grace reprimanded her. "If

people had any brains in their head, they'd cry all the time at how wonderful life is!"

* * * *

Saturday arrived and Eleanor waited calmly for Nathan. At the stroke of noon he was standing on her porch. She opened the door and directed him to walk with her around back. "Come on. The truck's in the garage."

Nathan admired the way she handled the truck, pulling it out of the driveway and out of town. "I've practiced like crazy," she admitted. "But now I think I've gotten the swing of it."

They drove into Gloucester, to Charlie's - a seafood shanty that served great fried clams. It had a diner-like atmosphere - linoleum tables and padded metal chairs - and it was a bustling, friendly place. "Bill and I used to eat here almost every week in the summers," Eleanor told Nathan. "I haven't been here in ages."

They ordered, and then Nathan couldn't stand the suspense anymore. "So tell me. What do you want to talk about?"

"Well, partly about the end of Gertrude's story. I know Peter filled you in on my trip to Lexington."

"Yes, he said that you met with Johnathan Flagg's nephew, a dentist. But he didn't know too many details. What did you find out?"

Eleanor told him the story of the end of Gertrude's life. When she finished, Nathan looked at her sympathetically. "That's a terrible story, Ellie. It must not have been fun for you to hear it."

"It was awful. There was still so much anger towards her. But Nathan, that's what made me realize just what a horrible thing she'd done. Johnathan Flagg really loved her, and she never gave him a chance."

Nathan looked at her expectantly. "Is this where I come in?"

"It is, but not the way you think. You see, I believed that Gertrude's love for Will was perfect, just like I believed that my love for Bill was perfect. And I believed that true love meant you could never love anyone else, at least not the same way. Well, Gertrude took that idea to its extreme, and look what happened. It helped me clarify some things in my own head."

"Like what?"

"Like that maybe Bill would want me to be happy, and if that means letting another person into my heart then I shouldn't be afraid of that."

"I agree."

"For obvious reasons," Eleanor said, teasing him. "However, I've learned something else as well."

"Uh-oh. What's that?"

"That for years I've been afraid to be my own person, to take control of my own life. Frankly, to be an adult. I let Bill lead my life, and when he died, I was lost. Now is my chance, Nathan, to become a whole person - someone Peter can rely on, someone I can be proud of, someone who is not afraid. I have to take the time to do that, Nathan. If I get involved with you right now, I'll never do it."

Nathan was silent for a moment. "So, where does that leave us?"

Eleanor took a deep breath. It was hard for her to say what she wanted, and she found herself looking down at her hands as she spoke. "I want to keep our relationship relatively platonic this summer. Then I'm going back to Boston to work out some things on my own. If I feel ready for it next summer, I'd like to start dating you again then." She glanced up at him nervously. "If you still want to, of course."

Nathan smiled.

"Are you mad at me?" Eleanor asked him.

Nathan reached and put his hands over hers. "Ellie, I told you once you would become someone extraordinary. Of course I'm not mad. You're perfect. That is just what you should do. I'm only glad you're going to let me see you again at the end of the process."

"Well, remember - there are no promises. I want to do this right. I don't want you to date the old me; I want you to date the new, improved version! So, however long that takes..."

"However long that takes," Nathan concurred.

Their food arrived, and they began to eat. "There's just one thing, Ellie," Nathan told her. "I don't know how I'm going to resist kissing you."

"Oh, you'll manage," Eleanor replied, flashing him her most charming smile.

* * * *

Eleanor was waiting outside the Historical Society promptly at two p.m. the following Monday afternoon. Gabby arrived only minutes behind her to unlock the door. "Where have you been?" Eleanor asked her. "I've been calling you for days."

"Really? What happened? Dad and I were visiting cousins in Maine."

Eleanor told Gabby the whole story of her trip to Lexington, and what she'd learned about Gertrude. "Oh, Eleanor!" she exclaimed at the end, "how awful!"

"I'm getting over it now. I definitely figured out what I was supposed to learn, at least."

"What was it?"

"Well, to put it very bluntly, to grow up. You'll find this hard to believe at your age, Gabby, but not everyone older than you is wiser."

"Oh, I believe it! I've already seen too many unfortunate examples! But you look happy, Eleanor," she noted, eyeing her critically, "so this lesson obviously agrees with you."

"Time will tell. I'm still walking on eggshells. I just keep telling myself to be confident and keep going, and to my surprise, it's working."

"That's called a self-fulfilling prophecy."

"Yes, I guess it is. Now, I have a question for you."

"Shoot."

"If I wanted to do a lot of research here, could I get access other than Monday afternoons and Thursday evenings?"

"Sure! I'll have to check with my Dad, but I'm sure he'll let me give you a key. What do you want to research?"

Eleanor told her, and Gabby's eyes grew wide. "I knew it!" she exclaimed. "Just remember who told you to in the first place..."

Eleanor and Peter planned the party together. She took him to the florist's, and let him pick out whatever flowers he liked to fill the vases back home. They baked cookies, and decorated them with jimmies and cinnamon dots. Eleanor taught Peter how to mix Bill's favorite punch - juice, sparkling soda and sherbet. They even prepared the finger sandwiches together, and when Peter had trouble cutting the sandwiches in pinwheels, they decided to consider his sandwiches "circles" instead. They laughed a great deal while they worked.

The get-together was a success. Eleanor was pleased to see Grace and Miranda make a fuss over Samuel Hopstedder, and hoped it was the beginning of his new social life. Nathan kept Peter and his friends spellbound with tales of old Annisquam, which Gabby often interrupted to embellish with her own two-cents worth of research. Everyone gobbled up the finger sandwiches and cookies.

Halfway through the party, Eleanor lifted her glass of punch and proposed a toast. "To Gertrude!" she exclaimed, and everyone cheered.

"What are you going to do with the letters now that you've solved the mystery?" someone asked her.

"You'll see!" she replied, and that was all she would tell them. But Gabby gave her a knowing smile.

Eleanor and Gabby spent a lot of time together through the rest of the summer. The younger woman became Eleanor's unofficial research assistant, and kept her supplied with interesting tidbits and details that crossed the Historical Society desk. By the end of the season they were best friends. Every now and again, Eleanor found herself wondering if Gabby really was Lizzie.

In August, Eleanor finished an article on Gertrude's letters. She sent it off to Brian Suskind, with a cover letter asking him to advise her on its publishability. She heard from him in October, when she was back in Boston. He had found a publisher for her article - a small scholarly journal that specialized in Women's Studies. After additional research and a few rounds of editing, the article was published in February. Eleanor sent everyone in Annisquam a copy.

Nathan saw a lot of Eleanor that summer, but usually when Peter was around too. The three of them went sailing, or swimming, or to the movies. Occasionally, just Nathan and Eleanor went out to dinner, and Nathan was careful to restrain himself from grabbing and kissing her. The trouble he had avoiding it made Eleanor laugh, and a few times she almost broke down herself and kissed him. They agreed to telephone faithfully over the winter months.

On her last day in Annisquam, Eleanor stopped at Grace's house to say good-bye. She found the older woman in the backyard, sitting in a lawn chair in the middle of her garden and surveying the summer's blooms. "Not too bad a season," she observed to Eleanor, as she approached. "We didn't lose too much to beetles this year."

"I came to say good-bye," Eleanor told her.

"Already! The summer flies by every year, doesn't it? Now, you will be back again next summer, won't you?"

"Absolutely. I promise."

"Good. Well, sit down for a moment! You don't have to go this minute, do you?"

Eleanor admitted that she had some time, and pulled up another chair.

"You know, Ellie, I've been thinking a lot about you lately."

"You have?" Eleanor asked, surprised.

"Oh yes. You have really grown, Eleanor."

It was the first time Grace had ever called her Eleanor, and Eleanor knew what it meant. "Grace," she said quietly, "I haven't changed as much as you think. I just act differently. Inside, I'm still scared."

To her surprise, Grace chuckled. "Don't you know that we all are, dear? The secret to life, Ellie, is not in the feeling. It's in the doing."

"In other words, don't let your fears paralyze you."

"Exactly."

"I guess I have learned that much."

"Of course you have," Grace informed her with authority. "I understand that you're extraordinary."

Eleanor flushed, then burst out laughing, and Grace joined her.

Epilogue

Nathan was sitting in his study, trying to grade papers but thinking more about the soft spring air outside, and the fact that Eleanor and Peter would be back for the summer in a few weeks. The doorbell rang. Nathan went to the door, and saw the UPS man waving as he pulled his truck away. A box had been left on his doorstep.

Nathan brought the package inside and looked at the return address. It was from a publishing company. *Probably a sample textbook*, he thought.

He opened the box and discovered that there was a book inside, but not a textbook - a novel. It was titled Gertrude's Letters, and the author was Eleanor Strayer. Nathan let out a whistle, and grinned from ear to ear. "She never said a word!" he exclaimed out loud, shaking his head in amazement. "Incredible!"

He eagerly turned to the first page and began reading:

Chapter One: Annisquam, 1883

Along the ridge of a hill overlooking the beach, a lone artist made his way toward the town of Annisquam, carrying an easel and paint box as he walked through the long shadows of early evening. He had spent all day concentrating, trying to "see" nature - to be one with his surroundings - and was now aware of a comfortable feeling of exhaustion from a good day's work. His mind was clear of conscious thought.

As he neared town, sounds of activity from the

beach began floating up the hill. A buzz of excitement indicated that something unusual was occurring. When the noise reached the artist, he made his way to the edge of the ridge and peered down.

On a wide expanse of sand just a short distance below him, a baseball game was underway....

"Thatta girl," Nathan said to himself, glowing with pride. "I knew you were extraordinary!"

Author's Note

The story of Gertrude and William Picknell is true, as are many of the details about their life together. William Lamb Picknell was a very well known artist in the late nineteenth century. His style was unique in American painting - it involved using bright sunlight to heighten the objects in his works, a style that has been dubbed the "glare aesthetic" by scholars. Today his painting can be seen in a number of museums, including the Museum of Fine Arts, Boston; the Metropolitan Museum of Art, New York; the Corcoran Gallery of Art in Washington, D.C.; the Pennsylvania Academy of the Fine Arts, Philadelphia; the Parrish Art Museum in Southampton, NY; the Cleveland Museum of Art; and the Phoenix Art Museum.

Gertrude did write to her sister Lizzie - probably very often - but only two letters survive; they are included in the novel but I will leave it to the reader to guess which two they are. Gertrude's personality and her tragic ending have been culled from bits and pieces of evidence that I found very compelling, even if not definitive. This novel has given me a chance to explore her character, without having to "prove" it, as one would have to do if writing nonfiction.

There are many people who helped me with research over the years. I am grateful to all of them, but a few contributed so much to this novel that I want to thank them publicly. First and foremost, Bonnie Ouellette, Barbara Johnson Wood and Jay Storer opened up their family history to me, sharing letters and photographs that I would never have had access to otherwise. Tom O'Keefe of the Annisquam Historical Society helped me find the Picknell cottage, which the Edgerton family and their tenants kindly let me explore. Barbara Ninness' help was invaluable - she even brought me on a land records search in Salem. Sandra Lepore in Newburyport first brought the photographs to my attention, while Terry Vose and Amy and Dane Harwood provided home bases in Massachusetts for my research.

Longtime Picknell fans Betty and Douglas Watson, and David and Mary Ann Chase, are always so enthusiastic about my work that I felt at times I was writing this novel for them. Their support of my catalogue raisonne project keeps that research going.

Finally, I want to thank my editor, Cap Weinberger, Jr., for his understanding and appreciation of this story.

About the Author

Lauren Walden Rabb grew up in South Brunswick, New Jersey. She received a bachelor's degree from Rutgers University and an MA from George Washington University. For eleven years she managed Hollis Taggart Galleries (formerly Taggart & Jorgensen) in Washington, D.C., and since 1991 she has been compiling the catalogue raisonne of William Lamb Picknell's work. She has published many articles and catalogues in the field of art history, and has taught art and literature courses at the Continuing Education Department of Georgetown University. She currently lives in Fairfax, Virginia with her husband, daughter and two cats. This is her first novel.

Photo by Cap Weinberger, Jr.